Welcome to Fortune Bay

I'm excited to introduce this new series set on the shores of Fortune Bay in Washington State's Olympic Mountains.

A ramshackle cabin on the lake is a haven for people at a crossroads in their life, where they can work through their problems with the help of friends and family, and with the occasional nudge from the friendly spirit of Aunt Augusta.

And if a romance grows in the process, well, so much the better.

Hope you enjoy it,
Judith Hudson

Lake of Dreams

A Fortune Bay Series Prequel

Judith Hudson

Chapter 1

Eight years ago.

Prying open the screen door with the toe of her boot, Colleen Murphy wedged her armful of boxes against the frame and squeezed between the cabin doors. She twisted the knob of the solid front door and gave it a thump with her hip. Didn't budge.

"Jake—it's locked."

Her brother followed her up onto the porch, carrying an equally heavy load and trying to hide the smirk on his face when he saw her trapped between the doors. "I left it open this morning, but it can be stubborn. You have to know the trick."

Colleen stepped out of the way. "Well you try. And make it fast. These are heavy."

Jake put his hip to the door and thumped. Nothing.

It was Colleen's turn to smirk. "Tried that."

Jake lowered his brows. "Come on Augusta," he muttered. "Quit fooling around." He hit the door again and this time it flew open.

Colleen look at him skeptically. "Augusta? Seriously? She's been dead for fifteen years."

Jake carried his load into the cabin. "Yeah, well, sometimes she forgets."

Colleen's eyes narrowed, then she grinned and followed him in. "You're kidding, right?"

He hitched one shoulder.

Jake had lived in the cabin off and on since Aunt Augusta died. If anyone knew if the cabin was haunted, it would be him. "Really. You're kidding."

"Well, there were things…"

"What things?"

"Little things. She'd hang up my clothes, clean up my mess, things like that. I heard sounds in the attic once, but that was during a storm so I wasn't sure…"

He set his boxes on the living room floor.

Colleen put her load down with them and rested a hand on her hip. "You could have warned me the cabin was haunted."

"It's not haunted. It's just Augusta. She's pretty friendly." Jake grinned. "You scared?"

Colleen tossed her head. "It would take more than a ghost to make me move back in with Mom and Dad. I was glad to hear you and Rena had moved out of here and into the farmhouse. Good timing."

Jake shook his head. "Rena couldn't handle living here last winter. The cabin's not really winterized. Never bothered me, it doesn't get that cold, but she wasn't used to the wood stove."

They grinned at each other and said, "City girl."

Colleen walked back out to the porch. "I probably won't be here next winter either. Unless I find a job in town."

Jake sat on the step and looked out at the lake. "Otherwise what? Back to Seattle?"

Colleen shook her head. "No. I'm through with the city."

"What about Kyle?"

"Through with him, too."

"What happened?"

Colleen joined him on the step. "The guy's a jerk. We were together four years and I wanted to move on to the next step. You know, a family, children."

"He didn't want that?"

"Not at all. Cripes, what a waste of four good years." She gazed at the snowcapped mountains rising up around the bay and sighed. "No, this is home and I'm happy to be back. There's nothing for me in Seattle anymore. I'll just have to find work here, or in Majestic."

"When do you start at the marina?" Jake asked.

"Tomorrow, bright and early."

Jake hesitated. "Doesn't it feel like a bit of a step back? Not that there's anything wrong with it," he hastened to add. "It's just that you did work there every summer all through school..."

"I know. I'll look for something in finance for the fall." The idea made her frown for a moment, then she smiled again. "I love working at the marina though. Being on the water, around the boats. Driving the lift to help Pete get the boats in the water in the spring. He's getting older, really needs the help. When he asked, I was glad to say yes. It's just for the summer."

Her smile broadened into a grin. "I even like opening at six in the morning. All alone on the water, a little haze lifting." She shrugged. "It's blissful."

Jake nodded. "My favorite time to fish." His brows lowered thoughtfully. "Haven't been fishing for months though. I've got to make some time."

Colleen looked at the lake lapping the shore thirty feet away and the cliff side of the mountain rising coppery gold in the afternoon sun across Fortune Bay. "I love this view."

Jake stood. "Me too. I hated to leave it. You can hardly see the lake from the farm. But now that the baby's here, we need the extra room."

Colleen smiled fondly at her once-little brother who now towered over her, his face infused with joy when he talked about his baby girl Sarah. "Remember, if you need a sitter, Aunty Colleen is right across the road."

Jake grinned. "You'll have to get in line. First grandchild, you'll have to wrestle her away from Mom."

"You coming to their place for dinner tonight?"

"We'll be there."

* * *

Alex Porter dug the oars into the water, rowing the old wooden boat around the point and into the quiet water of the bay. Built in the days of quality boatbuilding, his granddad's lapstreak rowboat might take on a bit of water but it was still a pleasure to row. He put his back into another pull on the oars, enjoying the slight burn in his shoulders as the blades met the resistance of the water.

There was something relaxing about rowing, facing backwards in a boat, watching the shoreline recede, the things you left behind slipping farther away with every pull. Two Merganser ducks lifted off from their hideout in the grasses by the shore so he angled further out into the lake. They'd probably hidden their brood of ducklings in the reeds. Next time, he'd bring his camera.

Leaning into another stroke, he lined up the center of the stern with the rocky point to guide him. It had been fifteen years since he'd rowed this stretch of shore, but as far as he could see, not much had changed in Fortune Bay. The log house on the point was still there, then a cluster of bungalows built by some mill workers here on the edge of town, the little white cabin set in the trees, a fallow field, then more trees along the shore.

Bracing his feet against the footrest on the bottom of the boat, he put his back into the stroke. He was a lot stronger than he'd been at seventeen and the boat ate up the distance. Getting back in shape was one of the things he was looking forward to doing this summer, his first summer out of the office since he'd finished law school eight years ago. The memory of freedom was beginning to percolate up through the crusty layers of sediment in his mind.

All at once he realized he wasn't going back to the family firm in Seattle. *Life's too short.*

The sun was sinking behind the mountains across the lake, sending long shadows creeping across the water. Majestic Lake was fed by snowmelt from high on the slopes and now, in early June, the water would still be too cold to swim.

Alex rowed passed a single-berth boathouse which if he remembered correctly, signaled it was time to turn slightly away from the shore to avoid running into a dock. He pulled one oar to adjust his trajectory and glanced over his shoulder to check.

There *was* a dock right behind him, and on it a woman with raven hair was dancing to a silent song of the universe.

He lost his rhythm, his oar caught the water and the boat began to rock. Resting the blades of the oars on the transom, he turned to watch the show.

Thud, she stamped one cowboy boot on the dock. *Stamp, clap*, she swiveled her hips.

One side of his mouth pulled up in a smile.

Stamp, clap, spin on her heel—

Her eyes widened and her jaw dropped when she saw him. Popping the ear buds out of her ears, she put a hand on the filmy fabric at her heart. "Cripes. You really know how to sneak up on a person."

She followed the rowboat with her eyes as it glided toward the end of the dock.

Alex's smile broadened. "Sorry. Next time I'll slap an oar on the water."

She put her hands on her hips and grinned, shaking her dark wavy hair back over her shoulders, and an image flashed through Alex's mind of a girl, thirteen to his seventeen years, standing on this very same dock, hands on her hips, appealingly bold with her almost-black curls and bright blue eyes.

She'd grown into that promise in the years he'd been away, and her smile washed over him, *like waves of sunlight...* He patted his pockets in search of the pad he'd forgotten at home. Too bad. Lines of poetry were as elusive as, well, a woman's smile, and were usually gone, hovering just beyond the edge of his memory, when he sat down to write.

He grabbed onto the dock to keep from drifting away. "What kind of dance was that?"

"Cowboy Cha-cha." She gave her hips a swivel and laughed. Tilting her head, she squinted down at him. "Don't I know you?" He saw a flash of memory in her eyes. "You're from the island."

"I am." He held out a hand. "Alex Porter."

She reached down and took it. "Colleen Murphy."

Then she straightened up and gave him a big, welcoming smile. "Nice to meet you Alex Porter. Welcome to Fortune Bay."

Chapter 2

Colleen stood on her parent's dock and watched Alex row away. She remembered him all right. Tall and lanky at seventeen, his curly sun-streaked hair hanging almost to his shoulders, his slate grey eyes so distant and mysterious. Not at all like the goofy local guys.

She'd had such a crush on him that one summer, always dragging her neighbor Louise or her little brothers out in the motorboat to cruise past the island, hoping to catch sight of him out on his dock.

An outsider, he hadn't been part of the crowd, although she did remember him hanging out with Dustin and Rory at the lodge. And wasn't *that* a sight for her barely-teenage eyes, the three hunkiest guys on the lake working and roughhousing on the dock.

Of course he was years older than she was, not interested in her at all. But just seeing him, even at a distance, having him raise a hand in a wave he'd probably have given to anyone who boated by, would send her into glorious fits of ecstasy. She'd been sure that in another year or two he'd notice her and theirs would be the romance of the century. That he would stay in Fortune Bay at the end of the summer because he couldn't bear to leave her.

The end of the story was always kind of misty and vague, but nonetheless thrilling.

She'd waited for him the following summer, and the year after that. Had been devastated when he never came back.

Oh yes, she remembered Alex Porter. He was still just as handsome as he'd been at seventeen, although now she thought she detected a subdued air about him. A sad look in his eyes.

His strong back and broad shoulders stroked the distance between them. He had put on some muscle in the years he'd been away. *Mm-mm-mm.*

Voices from up at the house caught her attention. Jake and Rena must have arrived. And Sarah. Colleen's insides warmed, melting like chocolate at the thought of her six-month-old niece. Line dancing practice could wait.

As she raced up the lawn to the house, Jake ambled down to meet her, Sarah tucked securely in the crook of one arm like a football. The longing hit Colleen hard in belly and she held out her arms for her niece. She wanted one too. A baby. Her clock was ticking. Hell, ticking was a weak metaphor for the heat she felt—an exploding time bomb would be more apt. Pheromones were shooting in all directions, but so far no guy had picked up the signals.

"Dinner's ready," Jake said, passing the baby into her open arms. It always seemed to be Jake with the baby, but then, Rena was alone with Sarah all day while Jake was at work and was probably happy to hand her off to him when he got home. And besides, he doted on his daughter.

Colleen didn't know Rena well. Jake had met her when he'd been away at school and when they'd moved back to Fortune Bay a year ago, Colleen had been working in the city.

Sarah snuggled into her shoulder as they walked up to the house. Her dad and mom were sitting in lawn chairs under the trees. Cocktail hour. Her mom's tall glass probably held a gin and tonic. Her dad was drinking beer.

He held up one arm when he saw her. "Hi, Sweetie."

"Hi, Dad." Handing the baby back to Jake, Colleen leaned down and gave him a hug.

"What's this I hear? My baby's moving out?"

"I've been 'out' for years, Dad."

"I know, but I'd hoped when you came back this time you'd stay with us. At least for the summer. Seeing as you're working at the marina and all, it would be just like old times."

"It's not like you're going to be around that much." She grabbed a cold beer from the small cooler on the grass. Her dad frowned. A web of red veins spread across his nose and cheeks. This wasn't his first beer of the night.

"I thought you could keep your mom company while I'm in the bush."

"I don't need company," Colleen's mother Stephanie said. "I have lots of things to fill my time."

Colleen sat in a lawn chair beside him. "I was wondering if I could use the aluminum outboard to get back and forth to work."

Her dad waved a hand vaguely in the air. "Sure honey, take the boat."

She smiled. Her dad was always a soft touch where she was concerned. Not so much with her brothers though. She looked around. "Where's Rena?"

"She was happy to have a few hours to herself," Jake said, his eyes on Sarah, asleep on his knee. "I brought a bottle. We'll be okay."

Stephanie frowned "A bottle? Already?"

Jake didn't look up, just ducked his head lower, dark hair falling over his forehead. "Rena thought it was best. She's been having trouble. This way I can get up with Sarah at night sometimes too."

"Not a man's job," his dad growled.

"Times have changed, Flynn," Stephanie said lightly, then, stood up. "Let's eat."

Colleen hung back just for a moment as her family went into the house. She scanned the lake, but there was no sign of the row boat. The curly haired stranger had disappeared.

Chapter 3

Alex cut back the throttle of the vintage Chris Craft and gently nosed the classic wooden boat up to the dock. For years after his grandmother's death, Granddad had kept up her tradition of placing lavish pots of flowers on the dock. Without them, the island looked forlorn. Deserted. Out of nowhere, a sharp feeling of loss overtook him, like a sucker punch to the chest that left him short of breath.

The lake house had been empty for five years, ever since his granddad had moved to a condo in the city. One weekend a year Alex's parents came to check on the place. He felt a pang of guilt that he hadn't come more himself, but his wife Liz had never liked it. They'd visited once early on in their relationship, when Granddad still lived at the lake, and she'd made it clear then that she couldn't wait to get back to the city.

Three years ago, his grandfather moved to Mooreland Manor, a posh and classy care facility. Not institutional at all, it was the best that money could buy. And money was one thing their family had in spades. Alex bet that his folks hadn't visited the old man more than once a month while he lived at the Manor, although they only lived a few blocks away.

Alex had visited frequently though, selfishly glad to have him nearby, especially during the last two, horrible years since Liz had died. He missed his grandfather terribly now that he was gone.

Flipping the bumpers over the gunwales to protect the wooden hull, Alex hopped onto the dock and carefully tied the old boat up. The boathouse needed staining, not really surprising considering the beating it took from the sun and the wind. A job he'd hated as a boy, staining the boathouse sounded good to him now. Mindless work that didn't twist his brain into nasty legal knots.

And fishing. He was looking forward to fishing.

He carried a load of groceries up the steep, rock stairs to the house. Being an island, everything had to come in by boat, adding extra steps to every trip to town, to say nothing of the climb up the hill to the house. Yet his granddad had managed to stay on at the island into his mid-eighties. He'd been a tough old coot, that's for sure.

As he headed back down to the dock, he heard the roar of a motorboat across the water, and smiled at the sight of the green and white hull heading his way. He'd sent Dustin a text saying he was coming this weekend. His old friend must have seen the boat crossing the lake from the marina. Or someone did. He remembered that from his teen years. It was hard to remain invisible in Fortune Bay.

Dustin pulled up to the dock and hopped out of the boat, clasping Alex to his chest in a back-thumping hug. "Good to see you, man. I saw the Chris Craft heading out from the Marina. Great to see her in the water again." Both men inspected at the vintage vessel. "What year is it?"

"Nineteen forty-six," Alex said proudly.

"Needs a bit of work." Dustin touched a spot on the hull with the toe of his deck shoe where the varnish had been rubbed away.

"She needs some work," Alex agreed. "She was Granddad's pride and joy. I'm planning to give her an overhaul. Refinish the hull and work on the engine. It's smoking a bit."

"Still, it's the nicest boat on the lake."

"I won't argue that. Want a beer? I think it's past noon." Dustin gave Alex a thumbs up and they headed up the hill to the house.

They'd been friends since they were kids, particularly since the summers Alex had spent with his grandfather during his teens. His parents didn't want the kids at home all summer, so for him and his sister Daphne it was camp or the lake house. Daffy liked camp, but Alex loved staying with his grandfather in the house on Majestic Lake.

He and Dustin had kept in touch over the years, but he hadn't seen him since the weekend fishing trip a year ago when Daphne dragged him up, saying she was worried about him. That time they'd stayed at Dustin's fishing lodge.

"When did you get here?" Dustin asked.

"Yesterday afternoon."

The men were silent for a moment, then Dustin said, "Sorry to hear about your grandfather. He was a great old guy. Everyone liked him."

"Thanks. It was a shock, although when you're almost ninety it shouldn't be too much of a surprise. At least it was quick."

"Yah." Dustin squinted down at the shore, paused for a beat, then asked, "Other than that, how're you holding up?"

He was talking about Liz. Two years since her sudden death in that damn car accident and Alex was still sinking. "Still hard. Maybe I've hit bottom, I don't know. But when Granddad died..." He looked down at the dock and shook his head. "I had to get away."

Dustin kept his gaze fixed on a family of ducklings down by the boat. "Don't blame you. So what're you going to do now?"

Alex sighed. "I have no idea." He just wanted to feel alive

again. He gave himself a shake. No one wanted to hear his problems. Especially not problems with no solutions. "So, what's new at the lodge?"

"Business is good. It's just the start of our busy season but we already have half the trip-dates booked for June and July, and about half the rooms for the season. Of course we only have the three rooms, but with breakfasts and grounds work, it keeps us busy."

Alex grinned. "Who makes the beds? You or Rory?"

Dustin's full lips turned down in a scowl. "We take turns."

Then his mobile features beamed with excitement. "We're expanding though. More rooms mean more money. I think we could fill another two rooms in the high season. Cabins this time, with little kitchenettes. They'd be popular with couples and not a lot of extra work for us. Thing is, we got the ground cleared last week and we already have our work cut out for us this summer, but then Matisse—you know Matisse?"

Alex nodded. Their fishing guide.

"Broke his ankle a week ago. He's probably laid up for the season."

"No."

Dustin gave a sharp nod. "Two months for sure. We're not going to get those cabins finished if one of us is out on the lake all day."

"Too bad." Alex wanted to help, but didn't know the first thing about construction.

Finishing his beer, he set the empty bottle on the barrel table between them and said, "Let's go see what's in the boathouse."

Chapter 4

Colleen climbed into the aluminum run-about at six a.m. the next morning. She took a deep breath, savoring the damp morning air. It was good to be home.

The sun already glinted over the peaks of the mountains surrounding the lake, making the calm water glow and infusing the faint mist in the air with gold. With one pull of the cord, the old motor started up. "Good girl," she said, giving it an appreciative pat. Sitting in the stern, hand on the throttle, she steered the boat gently away from the dock.

Cruising the shore with the engine low, the boat left almost no wake to disturb the wildlife. A prehistoric squawk sent a chill up her spine as a great blue heron spread its wings, wide as the span of a man's arms, to glide low across the water to its next fishing perch.

Undeveloped National Forest surrounded three quarters of the long finger-lake. Other than Fortune Bay which was built around the sawmill and Majestic at the head of the lake, there was only a scattering of houses, cottages and old fishing camps along the shore. Enough to keep the marina hopping all summer, but she knew Pete and Roseanne barely scraped by in the winter.

Turning away from the shore, she hit the throttle. The nose of the boat lifted out of the water, the rush of wind blowing back her hair, making her cheeks tingle and her heart fly. As she got closer to the far shore, a dot of white slowly became the store where Pete and Roseanne sold bait and a few groceries. At the height of summer, the marina was busy with kids and dogs racing up the docks to the store for ice cream and pop, but in early June the lake was still quiet.

Her heart beat faster as the details became clear. Three wooden docks stuck out like stubby fingers into the still waters in the lee of the point, the square float on the far dock listing a bit. The old gas pumps came into view and finally, Pete and Roseanne's white house, back by the road.

Pete was already sluicing the dock when she pulled in. She threw him a line and he caught it, securing the boat to the big iron rings hanging from the side of the dock. "Hey, Darlin'."

She hadn't seen him for three years—they had arranged the job by phone and email—and the sight of the sweet smile on his craggy face brought tears to her eyes. But as she got out of the boat and hugged him, she could feel his stooped shoulders and the frail bones beneath the soft flannel shirt. Pete had never been a big man, but he'd been strong, built like a fire plug. With a pang she realized he was getting old.

"Ready to get started?" he asked, pulling away.

"You bet." Unsettled by the changes, Colleen surprised them both by giving him a kiss on the cheek.

His cheek reddened where her lips had landed. "Enough already," he grumbled. Then his eyes softened. "We've missed you."

"I've missed you too. I tell you, working in an office from nine to five is not for me. Certainly not in the summer when the sun is shining."

He glanced up toward the house. "Here comes Roseanne to say hi."

Colleen turned to look, shocked to see the formerly fit, active woman walking slowly towards them leaning heavily on a cane.

"I was glad you wanted to come back this year," Pete said. "I hate to say it, but this might be the last year we're open."

She looked at him in surprise. "What do you mean?"

"We can't afford to be open all winter and we can't afford to close. The wife, she'd like to go someplace warm and sunny for at least part of the winter."

Roseanne had always been a spitfire. She'd helped with the business until the last few years when a bad back put her out of commission. Pete told Colleen over the phone that now, even in the shop, Roseanne couldn't be on her feet for more than a few hours a day. Watching her slow progress onto the dock, Colleen vowed to take over as much of that workload as she could.

"Sweetie." Roseanne gave Colleen a warm hug. "So glad you're back."

As she returned the embrace, Colleen noted that inactivity had added a few extra pounds to Roseanne's already ample figure.

"So, I hear you're ready for a change?" Colleen said, trying to put a positive spin on the words. "Maybe heading south for the winter?"

Roseanne smiled as she lowered herself carefully to the new bench on the dock. "Wouldn't that be nice."

"You deserve a break," Colleen said. "But what about the marina?"

"We're putting it up for sale," Pete said. "Claude Measlie is coming to fill out the papers sometime tomorrow. Best to list it in the summer, he says. People out on the water will see us at our busiest time."

He put a hand on one of the pilings that held the dock in place and stared down at the weathered boards. To

Colleen's way of thinking, he didn't sound as excited as he should.

"A new beginning for you?" she asked hopefully.

"I guess." He sighed heavily and frowned at the dock.

"We don't mind giving up the marina," Roseanne put in. "It's time. But we don't know where we're going to live."

"Hate the thought of moving to town," Pete added. "We've lived in this house for forty years. I can't imagine living anywhere else."

With obvious effort, he straightened, and put on a smile. "Guess we better get to work. The Hennessey's and the Andersen's are coming for their boats today. Got to get them out of storage, checked over, into the water and gassed up."

Colleen gave a mock salute. "Yes, Boss."

"You go ahead," Roseanne said. "I'll just sit here for a bit."

As they walked back to the warehouse where they winter-stored the bigger boats, the thought of selling the marina rattled around uncomfortably in Colleen's mind, but she put it aside as they got to work. Pete worked the fork lift and Colleen stood on the second floor deck, unstrapping the boats from their storage berths and guiding them onto the lift. The Hennessey's boat was a big inboard cruiser. She was easing it onto the tongs of the lift when a motor echoed across the water, heading their way. She glanced out at the dock but Roseanne was gone.

You could always count on someone coming for gas when you were busy at the warehouse.

I got it from here, Pete signaled, and she ran down the stairs and out to the dock, waiting as the boat cut back the motor and cruised in.

It was the boat from McClusky's Lodge, a logo of a fish

twisting on a line adorning the small wheelhouse. That boat had taken fisher men and women out on the lake ever since Colleen could remember, and she had filled the tanks more times than she could count.

But this time, when the man at the wheel raised a hand, his wild hair curling out from under a McClusky's cap, her heart started doing the Cowboy Cha-cha in her chest.

* * *

Alex fixed his eyes on the dock. *Can't be*. But one hip cocked, bold shoulders askew, it was clearly Colleen Murphy waving him in.

Mesmerized by the curves of the tight jeans and tee-shirt, he jerked the wheel seconds before doing serious damage to Dusty's boat and the marina dock.

Once he was in, Colleen grabbed the line. A few other boats were moored on the far side of the dock and he glanced over, recognizing the serviceable aluminum fishing boat with the old red Johnson motor that had been tied to her dock two nights before.

He jumped onto the rear deck, grabbed the rope at the stern and stepped up onto the dock.

"You," he said.

"You," she replied, her hands on her hips. Then she grinned. "Need gas?"

His eyes widened. "You work here?"

"I do." She opened the gas cap on the deck and inserted the nozzle.

He watched her work, wanting to say something, anything to engage those laughing blue eyes, but with his brain soaked in testosterone, he couldn't think of anything to say.

She held the nozzle to the tank and squinted up at him into the sun. "You didn't tell me you were working for

McClusky's."

"Just helping out."

"Got a tour this morning?"

"A big one."

"There's a good fishing spot off the point under the mountain. A good deep hole, pretty consistent, but there's a pile of rocks under the surface just this side of it. Be careful. That deep hull could scrape."

"Thanks for the tip. I know the rocks, and the hole. I fished this lake as a kid."

She looked down to screw the cap on the tank. "And now you're back."

"Just for the summer."

She stood up and wiped her hands on the rag that hung on the rail between the pumps. "Me too." She looked at the house on the shore. "Well, just working here for the summer. Then I guess I'll have to find a real job."

"What do you do?"

"Accounting." He tried to hide his surprise, but she raised her eyebrows, smiled and shrugged. "I know. Crazy huh? I understand numbers though, how they work, how to make your money work for you. In the abstract." She laughed. "It never seems to do me any personal good. How about you? What do you do?"

Alex looked out at the water. A fish jumped in the shadow of the mountain. "I don't really know. Between professions, I guess you'd say." He looked her in the eye, daring her to ask more, a strategy he'd found effective when handling antagonistic merger negotiations.

She returned his look, digesting the information—or lack thereof. She didn't back down, just nodded and let it go.

Interesting. Not the usual reaction.

"McClusky's are a good outfit to work for," she said. "Fair. Nice guys."

She lifted her shoulders and smiled like a child about to embark on a wicked adventure. "Whatever happens, I have a feeling it's going to be a great summer."

She handed him McClusky's clipboard to sign.

"Worms?"

* * *

Alex raised a hand in response to Colleen as she waved goodbye, then he spun the boat away from the dock, leaving a sparkling rooster-tail in his wake.

He tipped his cap back on his head. A great summer was just what he needed.

Chapter 5

Colleen stepped through the door of the Fortune Bay General Store and stopped to breathe in the comforting tangle of familiar aromas; sweet fruit going soft, smoked salmon in the cooler and above it all, the smell of Louise's coffee wafting through the arch to the café.

Fiona was bent over some paperwork at the cash. The store-keeper hadn't changed. Her dun colored hair was still piled in a knot on top of her head and the green sweater hanging off her narrow shoulders looked like the same one she'd always worn. When she saw Colleen standing by the door, she pushed the wire frame glasses up on her nose and came around the counter to give her a warm hug.

"You're back. Your mom told me you were coming. Maybe this time you'll stay."

Colleen returned her hug. "For a while anyway. I'm helping Pete out at the marina for the summer."

Fiona released her and stepped back, a worried frown pinching her forehead. "That's good. Now that Roseanne's laid up, Pete needs the help. It's too much work for an old man, and I hate to say it but we're all getting on." She hustled back behind the counter. "That dumb-ass son of his should come back from where ever he's gone and give his dad a hand. Family's family, I always say."

"Sure is," Colleen said. "Is Louise still here?"

Fiona hitched her head to the archway behind her. "Her usual spot."

Colleen stuck her head through the arch. The café hadn't changed either. Six swiveling stools with red vinyl tops lined the counter and two small tables stood by the window. Not much to look at, but Louise made the best muffins, pastries and coffee in the valley.

Her back was to the door as she scrubbed down the stainless stovetop behind the counter. Colleen put a hand on her hip. "Hey there. Almost done?"

Louise spun around and squealed. "You're here." Tall and thin, not even the harsh black clothing, long black hair and Goth makeup against her creamy white skin could hide the fact that she was a stunner. They'd been next door neighbors growing up and Louise had stood in as her little sister when they'd both had enough of the boys. Now that they were older, Colleen almost-thirty to Louise's twenty-five, the difference in age didn't mean quite so much.

Louise threw down her rag. "I am done. Just waiting for you." Coming around the counter, she sat on a stool. "Wait'll you see what I bought." She pulled a pair of shiny black cowboy boots out of a bag, tugged them on and gave them a stamp.

Colleen winced. "You've got to be kidding."

Louise looked down, obviously proud of her find. "How lucky was this? I needed some for the line dancing class."

"But plastic?"

"Patent pleather. Good in the rain, too."

Colleen laughed and tugged her friend's arm, pulling her out into the store. "I've missed you. Let's go. I've been practicing the Cha-cha. What are we learning tonight?"

"Tush Push."

"Can't wait."

The women hurried the two blocks through town to the Hall, past rows of small, brightly painted, identical square houses. In a mill town like Fortune Bay, the company owned all of the houses in the town site, a holdover from a time a generation ago when workers had no other place to live in the thick forests that lined the shore of the lake. Many of the families had worked for the company for generations, in the mill or cutting timber in the bush, and the slowing of the forest economy was of grave concern to all these days.

"How's work?" Louise asked.

Colleen smiled. "Great. I've been getting caught up with people as they come in for gas and bait." She frowned, remembering her unease when she hugged Pete. "I was shocked by how much Pete has shrunk though. I mean, I know he's getting older, but no wonder he's having trouble running the place by himself."

"Really? I hadn't noticed. I don't see him that much."

"He's selling the marina."

Louise's eyes widened. "Really?"

"I don't think he wants to, but he doesn't have much choice."

Louise nodded to herself. 'That must be what they were talking about."

"Who?"

"Two of my regulars. Independent fallers. They were in the café the other day talking about a big job coming up on the other side of the lake. They couldn't say exactly which property, but they had put in bids to log it with their crews next month."

Colleen stopped in the middle of the road and sucked in a shocked breath. "It's got to be Pete's property. There aren't any other large chunks of private land on that side of the lake."

Louise shook her head. "It'll be a nightmare. A big gaping hole in the side of the mountain."

They walked half a block in thoughtful silence.

"Have you met the new guy?" Colleen asked.

"What new guy? You've only been home for two days and already you know more gossip than I do." Working at the café, the heart of the town, Louise prided herself in being first to hear all the news.

"He's working at McClusky's as the fishing guide."

"I did know that Matisse is laid up. What's he like?"

"Gorgeous, actually." Colleen stopped in front of the Hall. "It's the guy who used to visit the house on the island in the summer when we were kids."

"The guy you had that big crush on?"

Colleen winced. "That's the one."

Louise cocked her head. "But?"

"But, I think he's kind of a drifter. 'Between jobs,' he called it."

"Well, maybe he is."

"Maybe, but that's not what I'm looking for."

"Are you seriously looking? After what happened with Kyle, I thought you'd take a break from the manhunt."

"I'm not looking for just anyone. I want someone who's ready to settle down. I see Jake with Sarah and my heart just melts."

Louise hooted softly as they walked into the Hall. "The girl wants commitment."

Colleen nodded. "I think I do."

* * *

A few mornings later, Pete was waiting at the dock when Colleen pulled up to the marina. His eyes were bright, his movements jerky. He was wearing his regular blue serge work shirt with his name embroidered on the pocket, but something was weird. Colleen looked more closely. The shirt had been ironed.

She climbed out of the boat. "You're looking pretty spiffy

this morning."

"The realtor's bringing a prospective buyer by. Thought I should look my best."

Colleen looked down at her cut-off shorts and the checked shirt she'd pulled on over her tank top. The weather was warming up, but the mornings were still cool. "You should have told me. I would have dressed up too."

Pete hitched a shoulder. "Won't matter. It's the land he's interested in."

She tried to keep her voice neutral. "What are his plans?"

"Not sure. Condos I think. We'll see." Just then, a shiny SUV pulled into the parking lot. "There they are." Pete hustled off the dock to greet them.

Condos? Was that what they told him? Colleen knew he couldn't keep working this hard, and Roseanne could barely walk down to the dock never mind help out. But surely they wouldn't sell to someone they knew was planning to log the land?

Three men got out of the SUV and Pete greeted them in the muddy parking lot. Roseanne hobbled out of the store and went over to join the group. Colleen drifted closer and started coiling a tangled mess of rope lying on the shore, hoping to overhear their conversation.

"Four hundred acres," Pete said.

Holy Cheetos! She hadn't known they owned that much land. It must either be a long stretch of shoreline or a big chunk of forest—or both. This was the last privately owned piece of land on this side of Majestic Lake. The rest was part of the Olympic National Forest and the national park. Together, their snowy mountains and deep forested valleys covered most of the peninsula.

Most of the land around the lake had been logged a century ago, except for a few privately owned acreages like

Pete's. What had been cut had grown back nicely—not as amazing as the first-growth giants, but tall Douglas fir and cedar. These days, most of the active logging took place much further inland, in remote, inhospitable locations.

Colleen snuck a look at the group in the parking lot. The realtor, recognizable from his signs around town, was doing a terrible job of hiding his excitement about brokering a deal of this size.

The other two men were strangers to her. One was short, slim and dapper. His impassive gaze slid over the land as if it was merely a commodity to buy and sell, glancing to the shoreline as the realtor expounded on the potential. *Condos*, she heard him say.

The other man, big and beefy with a red face, had his hand in his pants pocket, nervously jingling a set of keys as he looked up at the giant trees on the side of the mountain. The men exchanged a look and Colleen could almost hear the *ka-ching* of a cash register.

They weren't interested in the marina at all, or even in building condos. In horror she realized that Louise was right. They planned to log the land.

Chapter 6

Alex set his coffee cup on the wide arm of the Adirondack chair and stared out at the water. Cautiously, inch by careful inch, he let his thoughts drift to Liz, ready to pull back at the first sign of an ambush. But instead of the heart-wrenching pain he'd come to expect, all he felt was a pulsing ache. He blew out a cautious breath of relief.

For most of the first year after the accident, he'd been little more than a zombie, barely managing to get through the day. A nasty cluster of emotions—fear, loss, guilt, and pain—waited, stealthy as a cougar on a ledge, ready to jump out at him without warning.

People had offered to help, asking, "What can I do?"

But what could he say? "Hold me in the middle of the night," or, "Prop me up when I just can't go on." No one could say the words he need to hear. He'd lost his best friend and what he needed were intangibles, things that only Liz could give.

The night after the funeral, he stood in the bedroom they'd shared for five years and knew he couldn't look at the pictures of the two of them together on the dresser every day, put away her cosmetics scattered in the ensuite bathroom or smell her scent on her clothes in the walk-in closet. That night, he took his things to the guest room and never slept in the master bedroom again.

The next morning, he got up at the regular time, dressed as usual and went to work. His secretary Jeanine tried to send him home. His sister Daphne tried too, but his dad said, "Let the man work."

So he did. That day and every day since. Putting one foot ahead of the other, he got through the days, the weeks and almost two whole years. He kept working because Liz would have wanted him to. That had always been her dream, for him to be a lawyer and for her to be the CEO of her own design business. A privileged couple with golden jobs and gilded friends. Although he had continued to show up at the office, without her he had lost his drive to work toward that dream. He avoided social obligations, withdrew from his friends—their friends—and had not missed any of it.

The sound of the waves lapping at the dock soothed the ache that pulsed in his heart. He'd been angry for a time, but his grandfather had helped him see that there was no point. At first he wrote, a lot, but that stopped too as sadness and inertia replaced the anger.

He took a deep breath, inhaling the heady aromas of lake water and cedar, and a vision of Colleen popped into his head, standing above him on the dock, hands on her hips, a saucy smile on her lips. A spark of excitement shot to his groin. He smiled. He might not be dead inside after all. But the thought was quickly followed by a flash of guilt at the memory of Liz's smile.

He shook off the memories and tried to focus on the present. He enjoyed being out on the water every day. The fishing was good and working for Dustin gave him a reason to get out of bed. That was enough for now. Putting thoughts of Liz and Colleen firmly out of his mind, he went down to the boathouse. Today was his day off and for the first time in a long time he wanted to accomplish something.

Inside the boathouse, the tangy scent of fish and motor oil took him back to his childhood when the boathouse was a dark and fascinating world. Wooden hulls of his granddad's vintage canoes hung in slings on the far wall and three boats bobbed gently in their slips; the mahogany Chris Craft, the wooden rowboat and the serviceable motorboat *The Modern Millie*, named for his grandmother.

The Millie wasn't new anymore, but she was still in good shape. It was the boat he'd learned to water-ski behind and fished from with his grandfather. The boat they'd used to haul the old refrigerator to the dump and to bring the new one to the island.

In those days everything was an adventure, and just being back on the island had brought the feeling back. He awoke each day with a buzz of excitement, something he hadn't felt in a very long time.

All morning he worked on the Chris Craft, sanding the bald spots and covering them with a coat of varnish to protect it until he could pull the boat out of the water and refinish the whole hull.

After eating his lunch on the porch, he sat tapping his heel on the paving stones. For the first time since he'd arrived at the lake, he didn't want to stay on the island alone. Maybe he'd take *The Millie* to town to buy some groceries, cruise by the marina if he needed gas. Or even if he didn't.

It was mid-afternoon when he got to the marina, only to find it was Colleen's day off. When Pete told him the news, his first thought was he could have spent the whole day with Colleen if he'd known.

He headed back across the lake, hoping to spot her little runabout at the dock where he'd first seen her dancing.

His heartbeat quickened as he approached the dock, but no luck. Cruising slowly along the shore, he spotted her moments later, sitting on a rickety dock in front of the little white cabin. She didn't notice him at first, just sat, dangling her legs over the edge of the dock, staring into the water.

He idled the throttle and drifted in. She looked up but didn't flash him her usual smile, just quirked up one corner of her mouth.

He turned off the motor and drifted ten feet out from the dock. "Why so glum?"

She pressed her lips together and huffed out a frustrated sigh. "It's nothing. At least nothing I can do anything about."

He gave her a tentative smile. "Want to go for a ride?"

She looked away, considering the idea. Then she looked back and tipped her head to the side with a hint of that smile he wanted to see. "Why not."

Not quite the enthusiastic response he'd been hoping for, but he'd take it. He revved the motor and pulled the boat up to the dock.

"This dock doesn't look very steady."

"What's the worst that can happen? I'll fall in." She jumped into the boat and took the other front seat.

He started the motor and idled in front of the cabin. "You live here?"

"Yeah. I just moved in. It's a family place. Belongs to my mother."

"Nice."

She smiled. "Just me and Aunt Augusta."

"You live with your aunt?"

Colleen grinned. "Sort of. She's more of a ghost. I haven't actually heard her yet, but my brother Jake assures me she's there. I'm looking forward to seeing her again."

Crazy. "Cool. Ready?" he asked, pulling away from the dock.

Sitting back in the vinyl seat, she nodded.

He grinned. "Hang on."

He gave the engine full throttle and the boat lunged forward, forcing them back in their seats. She grabbed her hat with one hand and finally sent him the grin he'd been hoping for. The one that said she was ready for anything.

* * *

The nose of the boat rose out of the water, froth flying up to the gunwales. Colleen and Alex clambered up to sit on the tops of their seats, slowly bringing the nose down. She took off her sunhat and pulled back her hair, holding it out of her face with one hand, squinting over the windscreen into the wind.

Nothing could chase away her melancholy mood faster than a ride through the wind and spray. And a gorgeous guy next to her didn't hurt either.

They flew across Fortune Bay toward the town of Majestic at the end of the lake, staying far enough out from shore to avoid the log boom waiting at the mill for sorting. The sawmill sprawled across most of the prime waterfront in town, the ugly mess of old buildings a blot on the landscape. But since it provided most of the steady jobs in town, no one complained.

Once past the mill, forest closed in on the shoreline again. Sunlight sparkled on the water and the boat bounced against the waves, hitting hard each time. Colleen held onto the windscreen, a grin stretching her windblown cheeks. She'd missed this so much in her years in the city. A few weekends a year back home weren't enough to sustain her.

Fresh air and open water nourished her soul. Away from the confines of the office, she felt she could do anything, be anyone. She wasn't going back to the city. She was sure of it now. This was where she belonged and she'd do whatever it took to stay.

They passed the marina on the far side of the lake near

where it narrowed into the river which tumbled thirty miles on to the sea. Further into the narrowing channel, more docks lined the waterway and Alex cut back on the throttle. Maneuvering the boat around green and red marker buoys, he docked at an empty space at the bustling town wharf.

Colleen reached out and caught an iron ring on the dock. "What next?"

"Want to get a coffee?"

"Sure."

They climbed out and tied up, then walked along the promenade adjoining the wharf. Majestic was just beginning to come to life after the sleepy off-season. The kayak rental place had their colorful boats displayed outside, and visiting couples browsed antique shops and ice cream parlors. Families with kids would arrive in a few weeks and then things would shift into high gear.

The day was unseasonably warm and, as the afternoon sun beat down on their sheltered riverside table, Colleen stripped off her jean jacket.

"Feeling better?" Alex asked.

She smiled. "I am. A boat ride always does the trick."

Alex took off his visored cap, letting his hair spring free. Then he removed his sunglasses and hung them on the open neck of his Henley tee. His eyes were changeable grey, sometimes mild, sometimes stormy, his skin pale, as if he'd recently escaped from life in a dark hole. Colleen herself was pale after too many winters indoors. That would change for them both if they spent the summer on the lake.

"How's work?" he asked.

She realized she'd been staring, and grabbed her coffee, sending it sloshing over the rim of the cup. She hastily wiped it up with a napkin.

"It's really good to be back." She gave a self-conscious laugh. "I love being out on the water all day instead of cooped up in an office. Pete and Roseanne are like family. I've known them all my life. It's hard to come back and see how much they've aged."

"How long have you been gone?"

"Five years. I came back for weekends and holiday, but it wasn't enough."

"Are you back for good?"

"I am." She looked him directly in the eye, surprised by how good it felt to say it.

"At the marina?"

"Well, no. They don't have enough work to keep anyone on in the winter and anyway, Pete's selling the business." Her shoulders fell.

"Too bad. Might the new owners keep you on?"

Colleen laughed without humor. "They say they're putting up condos. That would be bad enough but rumor has it, they plan to log."

"How much property is there?" Alex scanned the forest rising up the side of the mountain.

"Four hundred acres. I hadn't realized until today how much land Pete owns, not until I heard them talking."

Alex whistled. "That is big. And heavily treed by the look of it."

"There are huge trees on that piece of land. Most of it is old growth forest. It would be a crime if they logged it, to say nothing of leaving a big ugly hole on the shoreline."

"It must be worth a fortune. I wonder what Pete's getting for it. I hope he got some good advice before he listed."

Colleen was silent for a few minutes, thinking over the ramification of that and the impact the logging would have.

"They shouldn't be able to log there, by the lake and so close to the National Forest. Isn't there some law against it?"

"I don't know, it's private land. That's not my specialty."

Colleen frowned. "What do you mean?"

Alex paused, then shook his head. "I mean, I don't know much about it. There must be some laws about what you can do along the shoreline."

Colleen leaned forward, forearms on the table. "Want to go and check it out? There's a trail that runs up the hill behind the marina. I know how to get to the lookout on the cliff. It's not far. Pete won't mind."

Alex pulled his cap back on, one hand tugging down on the brim. "Let's go."

Chapter 7

Alex brought the boat in to a spot Colleen indicated at the last dock at the marina. The platform on the end was listing a bit. "You could make a good living around here fixing docks," he observed.

Colleen clambered out and tied up the boat with a neat cleat hitch. He had to admit, she knew her way around boats. Little wonder, growing up here on the lake and working at the marina.

Pete was nowhere to be seen. Alex followed Colleen, off the dock to the gravel shore, across the parking lot past a long, open shed half-full of boats still in winter storage. Majestic Lake didn't freeze, and they rarely had snow this close to the water, but still, unless you used a boat regularly all winter, it was better to store it out of the water, under shelter.

Behind the shed, they passed a large building, closed in by industrial garage doors where the more expensive boats were stored. The Chris Craft had sat there, under a tarp for a number of years until Alex had freed it.

"Does Pete ever rent out workspace in the shop?" he asked as they started up a trail through the trees.

"He used to work there himself. Until recently, he was the go-to guy for repairs and maintenance in the valley. Still does some work for his regular customers, but I can see even that is getting too hard for him. In the spring, we used to put two or three boats a day in the water and he'd tune them up for the owners. Now he can only manage one."

"It is hard work. I was just wondering if I could use his

shop to work on my boat."

"*The Millie*?"

"No. My other boat."

"The rowboat?"

"Another one."

She turned to glare playfully at him. "How many boats do you have?"

He smiled. "A few. They are, they were, my grandfather's."

The trail became steep halting further conversation until finally it leveled out on a forested plateau. Giant cedars and firs, their lower limbs heavy with hanging moss, blocked the sunlight, creating perpetual twilight. Some trees were so large in girth that six men reaching around the trunk wouldn't touch each other's fingertips. Not much grew on the ground under the impenetrable canopy, but here and there an indomitable sword fern poked through the forest floor.

Colleen stopped at a fallen log, five feet in diameter, that blocked the path. It had obviously been down for a while and cedar saplings had sprouted up along its length, their snaky red roots crawling down the sides of the log.

At the sight of it Alex's pulse kicked up. He hadn't known this kind of old growth forest still existed in the area.

"We'll have to go around it," Colleen said and started picking her way through the forest along the length of the log. After a few minutes she stopped again.

"What?" he asked.

She pointed up to a low branch of a nearby fir tree where three grey fluff balls stood in a row.

"What are they?" he asked softly. The cathedral-like hush seemed to demand reverence.

"Owlets." Although she whispered too, the birds must

have heard her. They swiveled their heads in unison to look toward the source of the sound. "They could be Northern Spotted owls. They're an endangered species. You rarely see them." Pulling her camera out of her pocket, she took a number of shots.

Alex looked over her shoulder at the screen but it was hard to see the results in the half-light of the forest.

"It's hard to tell, because Barred owls are similar," she said. "They've moved into the area too. I can't say for certain which these are, but Barred owls are trouble for the Northern Spotted. They're taking over the Spotted's territory which, with the disappearance of old growth forest, is already shrinking quickly."

She took a few more shots, the owlets watching them curiously, then they continued picking their way along the fallen tree. A few minutes later she laughed and asked, "How big is this thing?"

"This is it," he said as they reached the shattered end of the log. He pointed to a decapitated trunk nearby. "And this is only the top."

They hiked back down the other side of the log to the trail and twenty minutes later emerged at a small clearing at the top of a cliff, overlooking the lake.

They peered over the rocky face at the steep drop. Below them, Majestic Lake wound its way fifteen miles inland through green mountains dotted with snowy peaks.

"This place is amazing." Alex looked down at the forested slopes on either side. "The logs would be worth a fortune."

"It would be horrible to cut these trees. They would never grow back like this," Colleen exclaimed dismally.

He nodded. "You're right. Once it's gone, it's gone for good." He checked the angle of the sun. "It's getting late.

We'd better head back."

When they got back to the log that crossed the path, he looked down its length, then at its girth. "Come on. We can make it."

Colleen's eyes narrowed and she shook her head. He laughed and started to climb the trunk using broken branches and new growth as handholds.

"Probably not environmentally correct," she admonished, watching him with her hands on her hips.

"We're just enhancing the trail."

He turned and reached a hand down to help her up. To his surprise, she took it, and held out her other hand too. Grasping her wrists, he hauled her up, her feet scrambling on the rotted wood.

Once on top, they looked down the straight, branchless length of the trunk, a feature that made Douglas firs so highly marketable. But this old matriarch was well past her prime, with ferns and berry vines and full-fledged trees growing out of her decomposing length.

Alex jumped off, resting his fingertips on the soft ground as he touched down. Colleen looked down doubtfully. "I don't know..."

He held out his arms. "I'll catch you."

She grimaced. He could see she wanted to do it herself, but in the end she sat on the top of the log and launched herself in his direction. It wasn't far, he caught her with no problem, and she rested her hands on his shoulders as she landed. He put his hands on her ribs to steady her. She looked at him and laughed.

Her eyes were striking, like blue chips of delft china in her pale face. His heart and lungs stopped functioning as he recognized the possibility of this, the possibility of another woman in his life.

Then she stepped away, said, "Thanks" and, tossing back her hair, started down the path.

He stood for a moment in the middle of the forest, inhaling the rich, moist air and watching her walk away. Was it a bad thing to want to move on with his life? Of course not. He just wished he could stop feeling so damn guilty.

When they got back to the boat, Colleen took out her camera and scrolled through the pictures of the owls. "None of these are good enough for a definitive identification, but I know of a guy who could probably tell us which species they are."

She pressed her lips together, thinking, then her tongue darted out and she pulled her lower lip in with her teeth.

Alex felt a definite jolt that time. Nope. Not dead at all. And more confused than ever.

"If I can get hold of him, would you come again too?"

He smiled at her, and laughing softly at himself said, "You bet."

* * *

A few minutes later, Colleen found herself alone on the dock watching regretfully as Alex roared away, her cheeks hot with windburn and her heart beat unsettled. When he disappeared from view, she made her way up the stony path to the cabin.

Darn it. She didn't want him to go. Not yet. Probably just as well, though. He was just passing through. Would probably move on when fall settled in. It wasn't like she was twenty-three anymore and could afford to have a summer romance.

She stopped on the porch steps and her spine softened as she stared, unseeing, at the screen door.

Regardless of how recklessly handsome he was, and the

way his wild, curly hair was totally at odds with those steel grey eyes. Eyes that were much too observant for a drifter and somehow, at the same time, so sad.

She pulled open the screen door and butted her hip against the wooden front door. She'd left in such a hurry that she hadn't locked up. It didn't matter. She had little of value, and anyway, she thought as the door swung open, Augusta had ways of keeping intruders out.

You couldn't live on a fishing guide's salary, and she didn't want to be scrambling for money when she started a family. He had mentioned something about the docks needing work. Was he thinking of taking on some extra jobs? Maybe he had construction background. There was money in that. It could provide a good living in the winter months.

Wait a minute! She hardly knew the guy and here she was planning their future together. It didn't matter what he did, he was not the one. What she should be doing was putting out feelers, maybe asking Louise, finding a steady guy with a real job. Someone already settled in the area, not someone who was just passing through.

But Alex could be an ally in the fight for the forest and that, she realized, was what she was going to do—fight to make sure the new owners didn't log the property around the marina and destroy that rare, fragile habitat.

Hungry after the hike, she put on the kettle and looked in the refrigerator. There wasn't much there, half a tub of suspect yogurt and some cheese that was turning an unsettling pink around the edges. She found a chunk of smoked salmon her father had given her and sliced it onto toast slathered in mayo. Add a piece of lettuce and you could call it a meal. She took the plate to the yellow Arborite table in front of the window and ate, looking out at the lake.

The lake and forest were in her blood. She was determined to take a stand against outsiders logging Pete's land, and hoped Matthew Swallow, the high school science teacher and local bird expert, could help. She had read some articles he'd written for the Majestic Caller, one about the plight of the Northern Spotted owls, and she'd heard he'd even written for Western Living magazine.

She decided she would call him tonight.

Chapter 8

Colleen spent the next few days dodging Pete at the marina. It left her feeling sick with guilt, like she was a traitor for going behind his back to basically build a case against the sale. They had to find out for sure about the birds though, because she'd done some homework and discovered that if the birds *were* Northern Spotted owlets, the new owners wouldn't be allowed to log the property.

She'd called Matthew, the birder, and he'd agreed to meet her this afternoon after work at the marina. She didn't know how to get in touch with Alex so she'd left a message for him at the fishing lodge.

The problem was, if they couldn't log, the perspective buyers might not want to buy the land at all and she knew how much Pete and Roseanne wanted to sell. The physical labor was taking a toll on them both and she felt terrible for sabotaging this offer.

But although she felt caught between a rock and a hard place, she kept moving towards the environmentalist cause.

She'd managed to avoid Pete all day but late in the afternoon he blew her whole strategy by coming down to the dock with a plate of freshly baked cookies from Roseanne. *Curses.* She had no choice but to sit eat them with him.

It was quiet, between customers, so they sat on the bench by the pumps.

After a few minutes, she broke the sticky silence. "Where do things stand with those buyers?"

Pete inhaled deeply and let out a whoosh of breath. "I don't know. The deal hinges on them meeting all the environmental regulations. It's not easy to put in a development on a lake this close to the park and the National Forest."

Colleen took another bite and chewed thoughtfully. "Do you think that's all they're planning to do? Build a row of condos?"

"That's what they say."

She let another minute go by, then, stomach in a knot, said, "There's a rumor in town that they're planning to log it."

Pete's brows contracted in concern. "I told them the community wouldn't stand for them touching those trees. Anyway, it would enhance their development to have a stand like that on the property."

Colleen looked out at the water. *So naive.* Pete had lived on the land all his life, run his business, content just to let things be. He had inherited the property from his father who'd bought it in the wild early days when land was cheap and the lake was a pristine wilderness.

"Truth is," he said. "Me and the wife don't really want to live anyplace else. But the buyers want the whole parcel, don't want to separate out a piece for us. They say it's hard to do, the way the land's licensed. They could be right. I guess they'll just do what they want once they own the land."

Exactly what she was afraid of.

Just then Alex roared up in *The Millie*, pulling into the space on far last dock where they'd moored the previous afternoon.

"Say Pete," Colleen said. "That dock's in pretty bad shape. Alex commented on it the other day."

"Not good," Pete agreed.

"He seems to know a lot about docks. He might be able to fix it."

Pete gave her a skeptical look. "Ya think?"

"That would help him drum up some work for the winter. People with boats would see him working here."

Pete was silent, so she added lamely, "I was just thinking."

"Is he looking for that kind of work?"

Pete obviously found it hard to believe. He must have figured out for himself that Alex wasn't a really motivated worker.

"I don't really know. He just mentioned it the other day."

Alex walked toward them down the dock with his rolling, long-legged stride, the gentle smile on his face directed at Colleen.

And then he could stay.

She smiled. "You came."

"Got your message."

A rickety old pickup truck pulled into the parking lot and a tall man unfolded his thin body from the cab. He waved a long arm at them, then reached into the crew cab seat and pulled out a back pack and a cloth hat with a floppy brim before heading toward them.

Colleen turned to Pete, the traitorous feeling boiling up in her stomach again. "Must be Matthew. We're meeting to go for a walk up to the ridge. I hope that's all right."

"Sure, go while you can," Pete said, offering the last cookie to Alex. "Who knows what will happen around here next year."

Chapter 9

Two hours later, Matthew's car disappeared down the road behind the marina. Alex turned to Colleen. "Want to come over for dinner?"

He hadn't meant to ask. No, that was a lie. He had. Ever since he put those two fresh trout in the refrigerator.

"It won't be anything special." *Damn.* He hadn't asked a woman out on a date in nearly ten years and he felt like a gawky kid again.

And from Colleen's blank expression, it looked like he struck out.

Then she smiled. "I'd love to."

Relief swept over him, quickly followed by a slap of self-reproach. But his lips formed a firm line as he pushed that feeling aside. He was going to enjoy this. It was just dinner.

As they walked across the parking lot to the dock, she said, "Whatever you serve is bound to be better than what's in my fridge. You've probably saved me from another dinner with my parents.

"We can discuss what to do next," she continued. Alex relaxed. Colleen could talk enough for them both.

"It would be so exciting if those chicks actually are Northern Spotted owls. Matthew seemed to think so—he was nice, don't you think? But they could be Barred owls, although, as he said, there haven't been many seen in this area yet.

"I'll follow you," she said, and hopped down into her boat.

Alex wanted to fly full-throttle across the choppy water,

the wind and speed matching his exhilaration about the evening to come, but he kept his speed in check, aware that Colleen, with her smaller boat and less powerful motor, might struggle to keep up. Every few minutes he glanced back and his heart pounded to see her right behind.

There was one brief moment of uncertainty when they pulled up at the lake house. but then he decided to give himself up to the flow and see where it led. He hadn't felt this elated in a long time.

He tied up at the dock and jumped out of the boat to give Colleen a hand.

"I knew your grandfather," she said. "He used to come in to the marina. He was a great guy, we all liked him. I was sorry when I heard he died."

Unexpectedly, Alex choked up. He turned to look out at the water, blinking away the tears.

Colleen looked at the faded boathouse with the peeling white trim. "He always kept everything so nice. Looks like the place needs a bit of TLC."

"Yes," Alex said, glad to change the subject. "I've got my work cut out for me this summer."

"Didn't he have another boat?" Colleen's eyes widened. "The old Chris Craft. She was a beauty. He used to bring it to the regatta." Her face saddened. "I guess it's long gone."

Alex smiled and motioned for her to follow, leading her over to the boathouse door. He didn't lock the house at the top of the hill, but he did keep the boathouse door off the dock locked, and used a remote control to open the garage style doors on the lake entrance. They were one of the few mod-cons his granddad had thought worthwhile, mainly to protect his pride and joy, *The Queen of the Lake*.

He unlocked the boathouse door and pushed the button to raise the garage doors. Light flooded the launch like a spotlight, bathing it in a golden glow of a sepia photograph.

"Wow." The word echoed in the hollow space of the cavernous building. "It's just as beautiful as I remember. Can we sit in it?"

Alex grinned. "Go ahead."

"My shoes are clean," she said, but still wiped them on the mat before stepping down onto the tan leather seat.

Alex grabbed the key from its hiding place by the door and climbed into the driver's seat. He leaned back, the sleek wooden sides of shiny Philippine mahogany encasing them in a pod of past elegance.

"How does she run?" Colleen asked, her hand stroking the dashboard.

Alex dragged his eyes away from her finger as it circled the chrome-ringed fuel gauge. He turned on the blower to clear the gas fumes from the motor compartment, waited a minute, then slipped the key into the ignition and gave it a twist. The engine coughed once and, with a puff of blue smoke, rumbled to life.

Carefully backing the long craft out of her berth, he eased *The Queen* onto the lake.

* * *

As the old boat slowly gathered speed, Colleen sat gleefully back in the leather seat. "I've always wanted to go out in her."

"I've only had her out twice since I got here." Alex accelerated slowly, treating the old girl with loving care. Her stately lines cut cleanly through the waves.

Colleen gave him a sidelong glance. His family must have money—or used to. So why was he working as a fishing guide?

They circled the island and he eased the boat back into the boathouse, trailing a light cloud of blue smoke.

"Motor needs work," he said apologetically.

"Can you do it?" she asked as they climbed out of the boat.

"I can work on the motor, and I'd like to get the boat up out of the water and sand down the hull in a few places, then varnish the whole thing." He pointed to the ten-inch-long scrape on the hull that he'd patched earlier in the week. "Someone forgot to put a bumper out and it rubbed against the dock." He suspected his father. "That's why I was wondering about Pete's big workshop. Whether he rents it out."

"I don't know. We could ask. He's certainly not using it himself anymore."

They exited the boathouse and Alex stopped and surveyed the boathouse and dock. "It does need some attention. No one has been doing the upkeep since Granddad moved away."

"Can you do that yourself too?" Colleen asked.

He grinned. "As a kid, I spent my summers staining this boathouse. Granddad had tanks and taught me to dive down and shore up the dock."

At the top of the hill, they stood on the stone patio in front of the house and Colleen turned to consider the view. The island was in Fortune Bay but the house looked away from the town and the mill toward the marina shore. "It would leave a big hole if they log all those trees."

Alex nodded in agreement.

Then she brightened. "But I'm optimistic Matthew is going to come up with something. He's connected. He'll know what to do."

Taking her hand, Alex led her up the steps into the house. At his touch, Colleen's pulse kicked up and a lick of heat touched her cheeks. *Just two colleagues talking strategy over dinner.*

And if you believe that, you're in big trouble.

The sprawling two-story house had generous rooms with wide windows to take advantage of the views. The furniture must have been of good quality when it was new, but now looked comfortably used.

He led her into the kitchen.

"So," she said. "Are you here alone?"

"Yes. Wine or beer?"

"Beer."

He opened the fridge door.

"Are you married?" She didn't exactly know why she asked. He just seemed married.

He stopped with his hand on the refrigerator door. "Was married. She died."

Colleen jerked back, as if she'd been doused with cold water. "I'm sorry."

"I'm getting over it." He set two beer bottles on the woodblock table. "It was a while ago." He gave his shoulders a shake, then looked up and smiled. "Bottle or glass?"

"Glass," she said, feeling inadequate to discuss such a personal tragedy, and embarrassingly glad to move on to another topic. She'd never known anyone her own age who had been widowed, couldn't imagine how devastating it must be to lose a partner, a lover, so early in life.

He turned back to the refrigerator and pulled out a plastic bag. "Fish okay? I caught a couple of nice rainbow trout today."

She smiled. "Perks of being a fishing guide. Sure. Sounds great."

As he washed and sliced some potatoes, she asked, "Where did you work before?"

He got out a pan and set it on the stove. "In the city. Hated it. Where did you work?"

"Seattle," she said.

"What did you do?"

"I worked in the conveyancing department of a real estate office. It was torture in the summer. I just wanted to be out on the water."

He smiled. "I know what you mean. Just a minute." He opened a door and stepped out onto a small deck where a barbeque was stationed.

Somehow they were back to talking about her. She tried not to talk about herself so much—it was a bad habit—but he was such a good listener she found herself rambling. Still, she had the distinct feeling he was dodging her questions.

* * *

Alex lit the barbeque and picked a few herbs that still struggled in beds around the back deck. Cautiously, he checked his feelings. Relaxed and—happy. He grinned. Well how about that?

"So what's next with this owl thing?" he asked as he walked back into the kitchen. "You must know some people who would work on it with us. Sign petitions, maybe come out to a demonstration if necessary."

Colleen leaned forward. "Do I ever. My mother belongs to a group of women called the Hiking Hannahs. They like nothing better than to get up to their armpits in local environmental issues."

He laughed as he started the salad. "Great."

"I'll tell her. She'll know what to do. The whole time I was growing up she was involved in one cause after another."

"That must have been great. A real role model." So

different from his own childhood.

"Sort of great. Her activism was always a bone of contention between my parents. Around here, more often than not, it's a battle between the environmentalists and the logging companies. And my dad's a faller. He goes away to camp for weeks at a time. He felt the protests were a threat to his livelihood. Mom, on the other hand, saw it as her civic duty to protect the environment for future generations."

"I see the problem."

"Dad hated her going to protests. One time, she actually got arrested and I was afraid that they would finally split up. Cripes, were they mad. Luckily, Dad went to work in the bush a few days later and by the time he got home, almost a month later, the whole thing had blown over."

Alex grinned. "Exciting childhood."

Colleen nodded. "Since then, I've noticed Mom tries to schedule her 'acts of public disobedience,' as she calls them, for the weeks he's away."

"Did you ever go with her?"

Colleen wiggled her shoulders proudly. "I've been involved in a few actions myself over the years. Once in high school, a bunch of us went to the local marsh armed with nets and pails to try to catch all the bullfrogs."

"What's wrong with bullfrogs?"

"They don't belong here, they're not native, and they're eating everything in their path from baby ducklings to native frogs. They don't have any natural predators here."

Alex smiled at the thought of her catching bullfrogs, but raised a skeptical brow. "Ducklings?"

"I saw one on the internet go after a cat."

He laughed. "No."

"Yes. He didn't get it, but he tried."

He started frying up the potatoes. "Did you get them?"

"Some of them." She sighed. "But it was hopeless. They were entrenched."

For a moment her shoulders slumped, but seconds later she was beaming the smile that never failed to warm him from the inside out. "We had a great time though, mucking around in high waders and canoes for most of the summer."

"Well, this might not be a slam dunk either," he warned.

"Maybe not, but at least we won't just be sitting around watching men and machinery decimate that beautiful piece of forest."

He nodded. "We definitely won't be doing that."

Taking the foil-wrapped fish out to the barbeque, he set it on the heat and watched through the window as Colleen poked around in the kitchen. This woman was amazing, but no wonder, growing up in a family like that with a mother who wasn't afraid to speak her mind. He was looking forward to meeting them all.

* * *

As Colleen nursed her beer, she examined the slate floor. Nice. A small hardcover book held up one leg of the kitchen table. Surely they could find something better than that. She reached down and pulled the slim volume out and looked around for something to stuff beneath the leg. Snapping an end off a small piece of kindling, she slipped it underneath.

Then Alex returned with the fish and they took their plates out to the screened porch that faced the lake. He was an excellent cook, something that in Colleen's estimation was a strong selling point in a man. He'd seasoned the trout with lemon and the herbs that seemed to grow wild on the back deck. Cooked to perfection, it flaked on the fork. The potatoes were crisp and salty and, while they'd talked, he'd put together a salad of fresh spring greens.

Although it was close to the longest day of the year, by the time they finished eating the light was fading.

"Must be later than I thought," she said. "This was nice, but I'd better be going. My boat doesn't have very good running lights."

His grey eyes, restless as a stormy sea, hovered for a moment on her lips before moving back to her eyes. "You could stay for a while. I could take you back later."

So tempting, but I'm not staying all night. "No. I'll need my boat in the morning. I have to be at work earlier than you do."

Alex stood up and walked around the table, took her hands and pulled her up.

Her heartbeat stuttered and all her good intentions flew out the window as he put his hands on her shoulders and drew her in, stopping when their lips were so close she could feel his move when he spoke. "Are you sure you can't stay?"

He was giving her a chance to resist, but instead she put her arms around his neck and pulled him closer until his body pressed firmly against her from chest to thigh. His soft lips met hers. They were amazingly agile. He didn't rush, didn't push, but the kiss was warm and thorough.

When he pulled away, she struggled to open her eyes. She leaned against him, her knees pleasantly weak, and wondered if it was too late to change her mind about going home.

The light falling onto the porch from the kitchen lit half his face and from this distance, so close she could feel his breath on her cheek, she noticed that the lines of tension around his eyes were fading. The death of his wife explained the haunted look in his eyes and it warmed her to think she could help ease his pain. He was obviously still grieving, and, she sensed, still vulnerable. Probably not ready for a serious relationship.

She would keep her distance, offer him friendship. Maybe getting involved in the owl campaign would help.

"I'll walk you down," he said.

Too bad. Decision made. Probably just as well. She didn't want to be his rebound girl, or whatever you call it with a widower.

She followed him into the kitchen, still wondering if was too late to change her mind. The book she'd rescued from under the table leg lay on the kitchen table. A slim volume, she turned it over and read the title on the front: *Collected Poems by Alex Porter.*

She winced. A weight, heavy as a concrete block, settled on her chest. She wasn't getting involved with another artist. Kyle, the musician had been bad enough. A poet was bound to be even worse.

Chapter 10

Alex watched from the dock as Colleen's running lights faded into the deepening dusk. His cell phone rang and he took it out of his pocket. He still carried it everywhere, mostly force of habit. He didn't get many calls these days. Just the way he liked it.

So he was curious about who might be calling now, hoping Colleen had changed her mind. But no, it was Daphne. His sister was an ally in family disputes, which in his family were often and ugly. But even so, his stomach knotted to see her name on the screen.

"How's the holiday?" she asked.

"Great. You should come up. Bring Geordie."

Since Daphne's divorce, Alex had wanted to spend more time with his nephew, but it had been a rough couple of years for them all. Now, suddenly, he wanted to teach Geordie to water-ski and fish, the way his granddad had done with him.

"I'll see. I do have some vacation time owing, although with both you and Dad away, I don't see how I can leave." Alex heard the accusatory tone in her voice. "Maybe later in the summer. Dad and Mom will be back in two weeks though and you'll have to be here for the reading of the will."

That was the last thing Alex planned to do, place himself squarely in the lion's den. "I'll try."

"Oh come on—"

"You can just tell me what it says. Granddad probably left everything to Mom. She was his only child."

"I spoke to Dad on the phone."

Alex's shoulders stiffened.

"He's furious you left. He'll raise hell when he gets back."

When Alex had left the city, their parents had been on an extended cruise. He was sure it had been his father's idea not to return for his granddad's funeral. His dad was bound to see Alex's departure as a desertion, ducking his responsibilities to the family firm, but Alex no longer cared.

"I got a job," he said.

Big sister's reaction did not disappoint. "What?" she screeched. Alex held the phone away from his ear. "You already have a job. What kind of job could you get in Boonytown? You are at the lake house, aren't you?"

"I am." He paused for a second. Better to just say it. "I'm not coming back to Seattle, Daffy. I'm not coming back to the firm. It was killing me."

She was silent for a moment. "I always thought you came back to work too soon after Liz…"

"Died, Daffy. She died." He could say it now.

"I know. But maybe this is just a delayed reaction. Delayed grief?"

"I don't think so. In fact, I'm happy here, for the first time in a long time. I'm busy and enjoy how I'm spending my days. I can't do this forever—"

"What did you say you were doing?"

"I didn't, but you know Dustin? And his brother Rory?"

Daphne laughed. "Oh, I remember Rory all right."

"Well I'm working for them. As a fishing guide."

"You're what?" Alex pulled the phone away again as if it was attached to an elastic band. "I'm just helping out for a few weeks while their regular guy is laid up."

After a short silence, Daphne said, "A few weeks?"

"The rest of the summer."

Another silence hung on the line, then she said, "I wish I could come up right now and talk some sense into you. But you'll have to come down in a few weeks anyway. Once Mom and Dad get home."

"I'm serious. I'm not coming back."

"For the reading of the will. The lawyer specifically said we should all be there."

"I'll think about it."

After he hung up, Alex shook his head. He was glad Daphne had to hold down the fort or she'd have been up at the lake like a shot, trying to convince him to go back.

The day after his grandfather's funeral Alex had gone into the office, seen the pile of files on his desk and knew he was done. He had been showing up at work every day since his wife died because he hadn't known what else to do.

Maybe it was the hint of summer in the air, barely discernible through the exhaust fumes that hung over the city, or the memories of summers at the lake churned up by his grandfather's funeral, but suddenly he had to get out.

In one day, he reassigned all his cases, closed up the house and left the city. Now Seattle seemed a million miles away and he wanted never to go back. But he had to find something to do with his life or, come fall, he may not have a choice.

He sat in an Adirondack chair on the dock and looked into the darkness. As a child he'd been a misfit at school and later a dreamer in the corporate world where everyone seemed to know exactly what they should do. Everyone except him. The only time he'd been confident of who he was, was when he'd been here at the lake.

His family had always expected him and his sister to follow his father's path, study law and come into the firm.

Porter, Porter & Porter. He'd never wanted to be the man in the suit, the man his father thought he should be. That was his dad's dream. It had never been his.

He might have been able to fight his dad, but Liz had bought into it too. Completely. He'd loved her enough to do anything for her, and her belief in him had given him the confidence to try. To show up every day and get the job done. Whenever he'd had a moment of doubt, he would remember she had faith. Then he would put his head down and do it. For her.

Since she died, he'd been increasingly confused about who he was. Sometimes he'd wake up in the middle of the night, or from a daydream in the middle of a meeting, and wondered where he was and why he was there.

All he knew was that inside, he wasn't the suited up lawyer he'd become working at his dad's firm.

Leaving last week had been a knee jerk reaction. He could see that now. After his granddad's funeral he felt he couldn't tread water anymore. He was going under fast and he panicked. He had to get away. Then he thought of the lake house. Quiet, secluded. Always a refuge.

Since he'd arrived, he'd felt like a clean wind had swept through him. Now a strange sensation thrummed through his body. It felt like—possibility. Change. He was finding himself, the man he could have been if he had taken the fork in the road that led to Majestic. He could make a change, do whatever he wanted. Whatever he decided. Whatever he chose.

Now he just had to figure out what that was.

Chapter 11

Pete backed the empty boat trailer down the ramp and into the water. Turning off the motor, Alex paddled *The Queen* the last few feet, guiding her between the rear lights of the trailer that stuck up out of the water. When he was in, he scrambled up onto the front deck and hooked the winch to the front of the boat, giving Pete the signal to gently pull her in. When *The Queen* was secure, he stayed in the boat as Pete put the pickup in gear and haul the boat up the ramp, out of the water.

Pete seemed happy to rent the big industrial workshop behind the boatsheds to him, and Alex thought that at this point in Pete's life, he was probably looking forward to watching someone else work for a change.

In the workshop, they put the boat up on blocks and Alex picked up the sander and began work around the refinished spots with long smooth strokes to even out the varnish. Later he'd go over the whole thing again with a lighter grade of sandpaper before applying multiple coats of spar varnish. Putting on a dust mask and goggles, he got to work.

An hour later his face and arms were sticky with a mixture of sweat and sanding dust, and he gratefully removed the goggles and mask. Nasty job, but nastier still if the toxic particles sifted into his nose and eyes. Grabbing a water bottle, he stepped outside and tipped it back for a long drink.

Colleen was down on the dock filling some guy's tank with gas, chatting up a storm. That girl sure could talk. She looked up at him and waved, then went back to her conversation with the guy, hitching her head toward the workshop as she spoke. Then she turned away as another boat pulled up for gas.

It was the weekend and traffic at the pumps had been non-stop all day. Pete did a good steady business in the summer months, and a pretty woman on the dock never hurt.

The guy Colleen had been talking to came across the parking lot toward Alex. A fit fifty-something, he was no one Alex knew.

The man held out his hand to shake. "Bob Foster."

Alex introduced himself, then waited for the man to comment on the work he was doing on *The Queen*. He did, briefly, then got right to the point. "So I hear you might be looking for some dock work?"

Alex's brows contracted. "Not really. I have all the work I can handle right now."

"I see. I was thinking of over the winter. My dock needs an overhaul and I could use a hand." When Alex tried to turn down the job, Bob hastened to add. "I'd pay."

Alex was totally confused. Where had Bob got the idea he was looking for work for next winter? "Well, if I'm still here next winter, we could see."

Bob nodded, as if he'd been doing Alex a favor. "Okay, we'll leave it at that then."

Shaking his head, Alex wiped the goggles clear of dust, picked out a new dust mask and got back to work.

A while later Pete came and stood by the door, away from the dust, watching. When Alex stopped and took off the mask, Pete picked up a tack cloth and walked over to the boat. He wiped of a patch of fine sawdust from the length of the hull. "Nice job. You know, if you're lookin' for more work, I could use a hand rebuilding that far dock. You know the one."

Alex allowed that he did, but before he could add that he wasn't looking for work, Pete continued, squinting at him with one eye half closed. "I'm surprised you're looking for that kind of work though, what with you being a lawyer and all." He let that thought hang in the air, as if hoping there might be a story.

Alex shook his head. "I'm not looking for work, but yours is the second job I've been offered today. Who told you I was looking?"

"Well, Colleen happened to mention you might be lookin' for winter work, when there's not so much guidin' to do."

Alex's eyes narrowed on the woman on the dock. "Really? When does Colleen take her lunch?"

"She's had lunch. She's in early so she eats early."

Pete called back over his shoulder as he walked away, "She's finished in an hour though."

An hour later, Alex made his way down to the rickety dock at the far end of the marina, where he'd parked his boat. Covered in fine sawdust, he threw off his shirt and plunged into the icy cold water. These mountain lakes never got very warm, but it felt glorious after hours in the hot dusty workshop. He swam out with long, strong strokes, enjoying stretching his muscles after a day bent over the boat. When he turned back, a figure was sitting on the dock, hand shielding her eyes from the sun, feet dangling in the water.

On his last stroke in, he grabbed her ankle and gave it a tug, laughing at her girlish squeal as she pulled her legs out of reach. Some things never get old.

He held onto to the dock with both hands and with one

strong pull, thrust himself up out of the water and onto the dock beside her, careful to splash cold water all over her, gratified to get a shove in return.

"What's up?" he asked, pushing his wet hair back off his forehead and feeling the rivulets of icy water run down his back.

"I heard back from Matthew. The nest is definitely a Northern Spotted. When he zoomed in on his pictures he could tell for sure. Time to rally the troops."

Alex laughed at her obvious excitement. "Okay boss. What's next?"

"Tell my mother. She's the real strategy expert."

Alex stood up, grabbed a towel out of the boat and began to dry himself off.

"Come for dinner," she said.

He stopped toweling and turned to look at her, brows raised. "With the family?"

"It's business," she stressed. Then an impish smile lit her face.

As always, her smile was contagious. "Okay, what time?"

"Seven o'clock? You know where they are?

He climbed down into *The Millie* and turned on the blower. "The house where I saw you dancing on the dock?"

Colleen laughed. "That's the one."

He started the ignition, climbed up to sit on the seat back, feet on the seat, and looked at her over the windscreen. "See you at seven."

* * *

As Alex pulled away from the marina, Colleen inhaled an excited breath and did a little Cowboy Cha-cha right there on the dock. Then she hopped into her aluminum boat and chugged across the lake to Fortune Bay.

She couldn't remember the last time she'd asked a man

to dinner with her parents. She hadn't known Alex long, but she felt it was time. Her dad was heading into the bush in a few days and introducing Alex to him was a kind of rite of passage. Not that they were really dating or anything. But it *was* developing into a summer…thing.

She stopped at the Fortune Bay town dock. One small dock, not nearly as big as the ones in Majestic, it was a good place to tie up to go to the General Sore. She ran across the road and through the store, hoping Louise was still in the café.

She was wiping down the counters and the stainless stovetop, but taking one look at Colleen's face, she stopped and grinned. "What's up? Who is it? The drifter?"

Colleen blushed, but tried to keep a straight face. "It's not a guy. It's an owl. In fact, a nest of baby owls. And they're the Northern Spotted. I think we can stop the logging at the marina."

"Are you sure that's what they are?"

"I got a local expert to come out and check. He said they were, without a doubt. It's time to tell my mom."

Louise nodded. "Pull out the big guns."

"Come to dinner," Colleen said. "At my folks'. I've already invited one person, I might as well invite one more."

"You don't have to ask me twice. I'll bring desert."

"Great." Colleen pulled out her cell phone as she headed for the door. "I'll let Mom know."

"What's his name?" Louise yelled after her.

Colleen grinned as she punched in her mother's number, but she kept right on walking.

Chapter 12

Back at the cabin, Colleen surveyed her meager wardrobe hanging on the rod in the corner of the bedroom. She was tired of wearing shorts and sneakers.

"And no," she told her reflection in the foggy mirror. "I am not dressing up for him."

Most of the clothes on the rack were more suited to a day at the office than an evening at the lake. As she flipped through the hangers, something soft and filmy dropped to the floor. A calf-length Indian cotton skirt, printed in colors of turquoise and yellow. She'd forgotten she owned it. And underneath it on the floor lay a scoop-necked yellow t-shirt she didn't remember at all. But what the heck. It was perfect.

"Thanks Augusta," she murmured.

She pulled on the clothes and turned from side to side in front of the mirror. Tight, but not too tight. She had a pretty nice chest, if she did say so herself. Might as well show it off. Maybe with her multi-strand turquoise necklace?

She rummaged under the bed and found a pair of sandals with a wedge heel. Not too high because, after all, this was Fortune Bay. Just enough to feel—special.

Her mother took one look at her and her eyebrows went up. "So, who is this guy?"

"Just a friend, Alex. He's helping me with a project." She wanted Alex there when she told her mother the news. "I'll just wait for him down on the dock. To make sure he finds the place. Unless you need some help."

Her mother shook her head. "I've got it."

That's what she figured.

Colleen kicked off her shoes in the back porch. The cool grass tickled the soles of her feet as she walked under the giant maples down to the water. The days were long, edging up to the summer solstice, the longest day of the year, and every evening of light felt like a celebration. Soon enough the calendar would turn and the days would start getting shorter again, but tonight the sky would still be light until almost ten o'clock.

The evening sun gave the water a golden glow. Sitting on the edge of the dock, she let her bare feet drift in the cool silky water. Putting her hands behind her on the warm wood, she leaned her weight into her arms, turned her face to the sun and closed her eyes. A warm breeze off the water shifted the hair on her neck.

This is where I belong. She wasn't going back to the city. She'd have to find a way to stay.

Her eyes were still closed when she heard Alex's boat come around the island and into the bay. Her lips curved in a smile. Maybe they'd find a way for him to stay too.

As the boat drew nearer, she shook off her daydreams and sat up and waved, grabbing the line as he pulled into the dock. He'd put on chinos and a button-up blue shirt, open at the neck, the sleeves rolled up to the elbow exposing strong, tanned forearms. She drew a shaky breath. She was a sucker for strong forearms.

He climbed out of the boat and up onto the dock beside her. He ran a finger along her jaw line. "You look nice."

Suddenly she was speechless, an unusual reaction for her. She smiled. Okay. So maybe she *had* dressed for him after all.

"I invited my friend Louise, too. She lives next door. And my brother Jake and his wife are coming." They started up the lawn toward the house. "There they are," she said as Jake and Rena came around the side of the house with Sarah in a snuggly on Jake's chest.

This was only the second time Colleen had seen Jake's wife since she'd been back. Rena was tall and thin with curly, shoulder length hair that flared in the sun with coppery lights. The dark circles under her eyes stood out against her pale complexion. Jake didn't look much better. Tired, his lips pressed in a hard, straight line, he kept shooting worried glances at Rena.

Even Sarah was fretful, teething Jake said as Colleen unzipped the snuggly and took her niece in her arms. Soft and warm and smelling like a summer meadow, the baby snuggled into her chest with a whimper.

"Poor baby," Colleen whispered. "Six months is young to be teething, isn't it?" She stuck her knuckle in the baby's mouth and Sarah latched onto it with boney gums.

Stephanie came to the door. "Oh good, everyone's here." She wiped her hands on the towel stuck into the waist of her paint-spattered jeans and came down the steps toward them. "And you must be Alex."

Colleen introduced them. "This is my mother, Stephanie."

Alex handed Stephanie the bag he was carrying, and she pulled out a bottle of wine.

"How thoughtful."

Colleen's dad came out the back door, lumbered across the lawn and looked Alex over with suspicion.

"And my dad, Flynn," she said. The men awkwardly shook hands. Her dad still felt he had to vet every guy Colleen brought home. And she still felt she had to run every guy by him. There hadn't been many in recent years, just Kyle the artist and, in retrospect, she'd have to agree with her dad's assessment of him.

Her dad looked at the wine and huffed a muffled grunt. Luckily dinner was ready, forestalling any more conversation. Stephanie suggested they eat *al fresco*.

"Why can't you just call it 'outdoors'?" Flynn asked. He turned to Alex. "Want a beer?"

"Sure." Alex glanced at Colleen.

"I'll have one too Dad."

Flynn frowned.

It was like picking your way through a cactus patch.

Luckily Jake stepped in. "I'll get them. Lager okay?"

Louise came out of the house with a load of dishes on a wooden tray. She put the tray down and when Colleen introduced them, stuck out her hand to Alex. "I've been hearing about you.

He shot Colleen a grin. "Really?"

"Oh yeah, the new guy in town." Louise blinked her kohl-lined eyes demurely. "I didn't hear it from Colleen, though."

Colleen stuck her tongue out at Louise from behind Alex's back.

Once they were seated, she couldn't contain herself any longer. "Mom. You know Pete's selling the marina?"

Stephanie looked up from her meal. "Just what you've told me, dear."

"I think the new owners plan to log the land."

Flynn nodded. "Nice logs on that land."

Stephanie frowned. "It's old growth. I don't think it's ever been logged."

"We went for a walk there the other day. We saw some owls."

"Damn owls," Flynn growled.

Stephanie caught Colleen's eye and gave her head a slight shake. Loggers versus Spotted owls. The feud had been going on since the eighties when the government began setting aside stands of old growth forests for the endangered birds. Although they had never talked about it, she knew which side her dad would be on, and it wasn't the same as her or her mother.

Stephanie smiled. "Your dad is leaving for camp tomorrow." She shot Colleen a meaningful look. *Don't start anything now.* "They're flying them in, somewhere in the Cascades."

The best paying jobs for fallers were in logging camps in remote areas. He could be gone for weeks. No point in stirring up trouble now.

She shot Alex a warning look. *Keep quiet.*

"What do you do for a living Alex?" Flynn asked, his shaggy brows low over his eyes.

"I'm working as a fishing guide for the McClusky's for the summer."

"Then what?"

Alex looked at him evenly. "Not sure."

Colleen felt a sudden need to jump to his defense. "Alex's had a book published."

Alex grinned at her. "You saw that?"

"What kind of book," Stephanie asked pleasantly.

Colleen hesitated.

"Poetry," Alex said.

"Poetry." The word exploded from Flynn's mouth.

"Of course, it'll never pay the bills," Alex said. "I'll have to find something else in the fall."

"So," Louise said, sliding in before any more damage was done. "You live out on the island?"

"I do."

Could you possibly answer with any fewer words?

"His grandfather was old Mr. Simpson," Colleen said,

pulling out all the stops.

Flynn's eyebrows rose to a friendlier level. "That so?"

"Alex took me for a ride in the Chris Craft," she added. Her father had often commented that it was the nicest boat on the lake.

"That so?"

"My Dad always liked that boat," she interpreted. Conversing with these guys was like pulling taffy.

"I have it up on blocks over at Pete's shop. Doing an overhaul."

Colleen exchanged glances with her mother and Louise as the men took over the discussion, talking auto-bailers and rudders and spar varnish. But at least no one was throwing verbal punches.

After dinner, Colleen came out from the kitchen to find Rena alone in the yard, bottle-feeding Sarah. Rena had hardly said two words all evening, and even then it was only to answer a direct question.

"How is she?" Colleen asked.

Rena kept her eyes on her daughter. "Fussy."

Colleen smiled. "Pretty young to be on a bottle isn't she?"

Rena sighed. "I had to stop breast feeding. She just wasn't getting enough. The nurse said she wasn't gaining enough weight."

Stephanie came out and joined them. "Every baby's different," she said. "We all just do the best we can."

Rena glanced up with a weak but grateful smile, then, head down, began gathering together the baby's supplies. "We should go." She shook her head. "I don't know how everything gets scattered around like this."

Her voice caught, sounding close to tears.

"Here, I'll take the baby," Stephanie said, scooping Sarah up into her arms. She gave her a little bounce as they walked away. "Let's go find that daddy of yours."

Colleen grabbed a stray teething ring off the grass and stashed it in the bag, then folded a soft pink blanket with a satin border.

"Thank you," Rena said softly.

"How are *you* doing," Colleen asked, feeling slightly awkward since they'd never spoken alone before.

"I'm okay." Rena smiled wanly. "Sometimes it's hard, though. I miss my friends, and my family, and my job and the city. It's just so different here. So..." She hesitated and looked around as if the answer was somewhere in the landscape. "Different."

Colleen didn't know what to say to that, so they walked in silence around to the front of the house where the men all stood around her Dad's old Buick, staring under the yawning hood.

Fascinating. Now if it was a boat, Colleen could have understood the interest.

Then Alex looked up and gave her a wink, and her knees softened like warm wax.

It was dusk, close to ten o'clock when Colleen walked Alex down to the dock. The sky above the mountains was an indigo dome that faded to aqua around the rim. The lights of the village twinkled across the bay.

"Well," she said with an embarrassed smile. "That's my family."

"It's a nice family."

"Yes, it is. But as I told you the other night, my mother and father don't see eye to eye on environmental issues. You would have seen a flash fire if we'd told them we plan to fight the logging. Dad would have hit the roof. Mom got the picture though and I'll give her the details tomorrow. She'll probably call a meeting or something once my dad is gone."

"Let me know."

They stopped on the dock by the boat. The water was still, without a ripple.

This time when he reached for her she was ready, and she softened into his arms, the growing dusk sheltering them from prying eyes. The man really knew how to kiss.

When he pulled away, she drew a shaky breath, then blew it out, overcome by the awareness that they could be on the brink of something big.

She smiled at the thought. "See you tomorrow."

He waved as he drove away. When the lights of the boat disappeared behind the island, the goofy smile melted from her lips.

She smacked the heel of her palm on her forehead. What was she doing? *A poet?* A poet who was obviously not over the death of his wife?

She groaned and sat abruptly on the dock. Then she lay on her back and looked at the stars, not ready just yet to go back to the house and face her parents.

There was no moon, so the stars had center stage. The dark sky and resulting star show was one of the bonuses of being so far away from the city. She recognized Orion by the tight row of three stars that formed his belt, and imagined his arms raised, cocking the arrow in his bow.

A board creaked and the dock shifted.

"Just me," Louise said softly, coming over and lying down beside her. "Always the best seats in the house."

They'd lain like this as children, all the kids in a row. Louise had lived next door forever, but had been more Sean's friend growing up. In the summer, though, they'd often all ended up lying on the dock like this, telling stories and counting stars.

"I miss Sean," Colleen said. Her youngest brother was away at college and working in the city for the summer. He rarely came home.

"He's the only one who knew anything about stars," Louise agreed.

They lapsed into silence. A few minutes later, Louise said, "So that's your mystery man."

Colleen's cheeks tingled. "He's not mine."

"He sure is a cutie. All those curls. No wonder you've been keeping him to yourself."

"He's a widower."

Louise looked at her, aghast. "How tragic. So young."

"I know. It must be hard. They were just getting started."

They lay in silence for a moment, then Colleen said, "He's not over her yet."

"I'm not surprised."

Colleen sighed. "And he's a poet."

"I bet poets make good lovers."

"That's not the point—"

"I beg to differ."

"No." Colleen was adamant. "I worked my butt off in Seattle at a job I hated for three years while Kyle worked on his art. He never made any money—not any real money, not money for us. Any time he sold a painting the money went into more art supplies. Anytime he got a job it only lasted a couple of weeks. I'm not doing that again."

"Doesn't Alex's family have money? They have that big place on the island and everything."

"I don't know, and anyway, I don't want a man who lives on family money. I want a man with goals of his own."

Louise laughed. "Well then, you can give him to me."

"He's not mine to give," Colleen said in exasperation.

"Oh, sweetie, I've seen how he looks at you. I think he is."

Chapter 13

The night of the owl meeting at her mother's house, Colleen's heart beat an excited tattoo as Alex's boat pulled up at the dock. She counted on his support.

He hopped out onto the dock and wrapped an arm around her waist, giving her a quick kiss as they walked toward the steady hum of voices emanating from a group of people sitting around a table set under the trees.

Colleen had mixed feelings about this clandestine meeting to discuss the situation at the marina. Louise had come over from next door, Fiona was there with her husband, a faller, and Matthew represented the bird watching society. There were a few other vaguely familiar faces, friends of her mother's, members of the Sierra Club who had already been working to set aside certain parcels of land for the Northern Spotted owls.

Stephanie chaired the meeting that was peppered with lively discussion. The trail up to the ridge turned out to be a community favorite and the locals present were all emphatically opposed to any logging taking place.

"Well you better get ready." Fiona's husband Matt said in a gruff voice. "I heard it's slated to go down within the month. Inspectors are coming out next week."

"They're trying to slide this by before we get a chance to ratify the ecological designation for the area," one of the environmentalists added.

Colleen sat in amazed silence as the discussion unfolded. Little had she realized what she'd unleashed when she told her mother about the birds. These people were connected and knew what they were doing. Before the evening was over they had formed a plan to get word to the media, both print and the Seattle television stations, quickly, while the element of surprise was on their side, before the prospective buyers got the okay to log the tract of land.

When the meeting wrapped up, Colleen walked Alex down to the dock. Clouds had moved in and there was the tang of ozone in the air. Her skin was electric, the hairs on her arms standing on end, sending tiny shivers through her system when her arm brushed against his.

They stopped at the boat and looked at each other. She wasn't ready for the evening to end.

"So, it's happening," he said.

"I know. So fast. We should find out when the inspector is coming. That would be the best time to hold a demonstration."

"What about Pete and Roseanne?"

Colleen shook her head. "I'm worried. I guess I didn't really think this through. Telling my mom has set this big crazy machine in motion. We couldn't stop it now if we tried." She wrinkled her forehead. "I do believe that logging that land is the wrong thing to do, morally and environmentally, but stopping the logging will probably kill the deal for Pete."

"It's a great piece of land. Surely he'll find another buyer."

Colleen blew out a breath. "We can only hope."

He put his arms around her waist and pulled her to him. She clasped her hands around his neck. They were in this together.

His lips pressed hard and insistent on hers, sending shockwaves to her belly and beyond. His hands slid down and pulled her hips against him. He dropped his lips to her neck and she arched against him.

"Let me take you home," he murmured between kisses.

The rain started when they were halfway across the bay, pattering on the canvas roof of the boat. By the time they reached the cabin, it was coming down in sheets.

Colleen looked at him with a mock-serious expression. "I don't think you should be out on the lake in this."

He nodded, a smile lifting the corner of his lips. "In case of lightning."

She knew that the atmospheric conditions in the Pacific Northwest made the chance of lightning almost nonexistent.

"Make a run for it?" she asked.

He nodded and they clambered out of the boat. When Colleen's feet hit the wet dock, they shot out from under her and her butt hit the dock with a splat. Alex pulled her to her feet and, laughing, they raced for the cabin.

Rain thundered on the tin roof of the porch. Her skirt was soaked and she cradled the wrist that had taken the brunt of her weight when she fell.

"Let me see," he said, and lifted her hand, studying her wrist before turning it over and kissing the sensitive white skin on the underside.

"Oh, you're good," she murmured.

He laid a row of kisses up her inner arm and when he reached the elbow, goose bumps rush the rest of the way to her shoulder. "M-m-m."

He looked up at her through ridiculously thick eyelashes. "There's more."

She grinned. "I bet there is. Let me get out of these wet clothes."

He held the screen door open. "I'll give you a hand."

She opened the inner door and led the way inside. He

gave the cabin a quick glance. "Cute."

Then Colleen dropped her wet cotton skirt onto the floor and that was the end of the conversation.

He did have more, much more, and as he backed her across the room toward the bedroom doorway, he showed her just what his agile lips could do. First on her lips. She put her hands on his head, winding her fingers through his thick curly hair as his hands found the buttons on her blouse. Magically, it drifted off her shoulders and down her arms to join the skirt on the floor. His hands moved to her butt while he kissed his way down her neck to her collar bone.

Oh my god. If this was what his lips could do to her collar bone, she really wanted to know what he could do if he moved further south. With her hands, she guided his head to the tops of her breasts, glad she'd taken the time to dig out the lacy bra and panties she hadn't worn since she'd arrived in the Bay.

They got tangled in the curtain that hid the bedroom door, and laughing, finally made it through. His shirt was gone too now—she wasn't exactly sure how—and her hands skimmed over strong pecs and shoulders, and vague thoughts drifted through the back of her mind that Kyle hadn't been built anything like this.

Her knees were delightfully weak by the time he backed her up to the bed and she fell onto it gratefully. He looked down on her, his eyes tracing her curves from the shoulder down to her panties.

"These are wet," he said, hooking his thumbs on the elastic waist. "They have to go too." And seconds later they did.

She reached back to undo her bra and then stopped. "Your turn."

When his pants hit the floor, she flipped open the clasp.

* * *

Alex lay on his back, heart pounding.

Colleen nestled under his arm, her head on his chest. She giggled. "Are you having a heart attack?"

He laughed. "Maybe. It's been a while."

She snuggled closer and he relaxed into the soft warmth of her body.

In the two long years since his wife's death Alex had hardly thought about sex. Until he met Colleen. Now it seemed to be all he thought about. He'd been worried he wouldn't be able to perform, but no problem there. He was back.

But what about her? Was she ready to take their friendship to a new level? He didn't know anything about her past relationships. If they were in fact 'past'.

At the thought, his arm, wrapped around her, turned to clay and his legs felt all wrong, tangled up with hers. He cleared his throat. "What about you?"

"M-m-m. It was great. Couldn't you tell?" She wiggled her butt under his hand.

Even as he hardened for her again, warning bells clanged in his head. He was falling over the edge for this woman and he didn't think he was strong enough yet to make it if she wasn't going over too.

He pulled his hand away and struggled to sit up on the bed, not an easy task on the soft, old mattress. "No. I mean, is there anyone else?"

She twisted her head and gave him a squinty-eyed glare. Then hitched herself up, plumping two pillows behind her back and pulling the sheet demurely over her chest. "Do you think I'd jump into bed with you if there was someone else?"

"Well no, of course not." But she hadn't answered the question.

She turned her head and gave him an angry frown.

Well shit, how was he supposed to know? People did it all the time. Maybe not him, but people. He knew better than to say that though. Not when she was looking at him that way.

She glanced away and said, "There was someone until recently. Quite recently. Very recently."

So, he was her rebound guy. Recipe for disaster. His heart deflated in his chest.

"When I came back here last month it was a complete break. I haven't seen him since and don't want to."

She looked at him again. "He was an artist too."

"What do you mean, 'too'?"

"He was an artist, you're a poet. To tell you the truth, I was worried it would be the same thing all over again." She flounced the sheets, arranging them around her.

"That's not fair."

"Well it's the truth. I tried to get you work—"

"Dock work."

"Yes."

"I knew it was you. What made you think I want to fix docks?"

She pressed her lips together, silent for a moment. "I thought if you had work for the winter you might...stay."

"Well I might stay anyway."

"And do what? Live off your parent's money? I'm pretty sure you can't live on what you make as a poet."

Okay. Now he was mad. He had plenty of skills besides lawyering, and he wasn't going to tell her about *that* because he didn't plan to be forced into that life by a woman again.

He stopped. Is that how he'd felt about Liz? That she *forced* him to be a lawyer? He'd loved her a lot, always would, but now that he'd begun to find his own way, he wasn't going to have some bossy woman he hardly knew try to tell him what to do with his life.

He swung his legs over the side of the bed. Better not to talk until he'd figured out what to say.

"I'd better go. It's been—" What? Fun? Great? Life affirming? "Nice."

She sucked in a breath. "Nice?"

Great. Now she was furious. Alex pulled on his pants. *Get out, quick, before things get any worse.*

He found his shirt thrown across the couch and as he pulled it on, he tried to make a gracious exit. "I mean it. It was great. Thank you. We'll talk soon." If she ever spoke to him again. But right now he just had to get out.

The rain had stopped, but with no moon or stars, the lake was a dark hole in the landscape. He put on his running lights and aimed the boat for the island.

How, in a matter of minutes, had everything crumbled like that? Gone from mind numbing satisfaction to anger and harsh words.

It was probably his fault. He hadn't meant to be abrupt. He'd just panicked. He obviously wasn't ready for this. He'd thought he was, but truthfully, he was still mucking about waist deep in doubt. And until he had his life on track, until he knew which damn track he was on, he was better off going it alone.

Too bad. The vision of Colleen, seductive and sensual on the rough cabin bed, would haunt his dreams for a long time to come.

As he climbed the hill to the dark, empty lake house, the phone in his pocket rang.

It was Daphne. "Hey Alex. It's time. They want to read the will on Thursday morning, and they want you here."

Perfect timing. "I'll be there tomorrow night."

Chapter 14

Two days later, Colleen sat beside Pete on the bench by the water, stiff as a statue, as if the slightest movement would give her away. Her anxiety about the marina land had been increasing steadily since the meeting at her mom's.

Anxiety? Call it what it is. Guilt.

The sky was overcast with occasional squalls ruffling the surface of the lake. Few people were out on the water and they hadn't had a customer for hours.

"The EPA Inspector is coming next Tuesday," Pete said. "Made an appointment."

Tuesday, that was five days away. She'd pass the information on to her mother, but she'd feel like a traitor doing it.

Her stomach churned; she couldn't keep up this duplicity. Pete deserved to know what was coming. "The community will be in an uproar if they try to log this land."

"I know. I told 'em."

"What will you do if this deal falls through?"

"Don't know. Hang on here as long as we can, I guess. I don't have a plan B."

He looked around. "I hate to leave it though. This place has been my life."

Colleen scanned the forest rising to the ridge behind them. "What if they found some, say, owls in there." Her voice was almost a whisper. Everyone on the peninsula knew what that meant. The battle between the loggers and environmentalists had been raging for years.

"Well, that'd put the kibosh on it."

She chewed on her lip and glanced at Pete. He was looking up at the mountain too. "We saw them."

Emotions filtered across his craggy features. Surprise. Disbelief. Understanding. "Owls?"

Colleen nodded. "Northern Spotted," she said softly.

He closed his eyes and shook his head. "Well, that pretty much seals the deal then."

"It's not for sure. Not yet." Was she trying to soften the blow? She wanted everything to work out for both Pete and the owls, but couldn't see how to combine those two outcomes.

She wanted to talk to Alex, but he hadn't been by the marina since two nights ago when he had stormed out the cabin door.

That had all just been a big misunderstanding. Was he really going to be this stubborn? If so, she didn't see them going anywhere.

But she really wanted to talk to him now.

* * *

When Alex arrived in Seattle, he went straight to his house. He could have gone to Daphne's, she'd phoned to invite him, but he wanted to be alone, to think.

He'd left things in a mess up at the lake. Colleen was mad at him and Pete was in danger of losing the deal on his property. Alex had seen how hard it was for Pete to drag himself through the work at the marina every day and he felt like a heel for his part in instigating the public backlash against the sale. But when he thought back to the special, almost sacred feeling he'd had when they'd walked through that ancient forest and found the owls, he knew it was the right thing to do. Still, he wished there was some way to mitigate the damage to Pete's retirement plans.

The house was dark and cool when he let himself in. He'd been gone for three weeks. *Really?* It seemed like a lifetime. The house cleaner had been by and everything was in order. A sterile, almost institutional kind of order. No wonder he felt brain dead when he'd lived there alone. There was no visual stimulation, no apparent hobbies or interests. No boat in the basement to work on while he thought.

He glanced out the back patio doors. The cover on the pool was on tight. A note stuck in the screen door showed that the maintenance man had been by too. He had never used the pool. What was the point? It wasn't a substitute for the lake.

When he'd been up at the lake he had wondered if, when he came back, he would slip into the old pattern. If he'd feel like going to the office to see how things were going. But what things? He didn't care about any of the cases, didn't really have any friends there. Not one person from work had called him the whole time he'd been away. Of course, that was his own fault. After Liz died he became a recluse, turning down social invitations until they stopped coming, and then feeling relieved to be left alone.

Now, though, the coldness of his house made him uneasy, his echoing footsteps intensifying the silence.

He put his duffle bag in the spare room—his room—and walked down the hall to the master. Opening the door, he stood in the doorway. He hadn't stepped inside this room since he'd moved out the night after his wife's funeral. Now he put a tentative foot inside the door. When he wasn't struck by lightning, he took another step, and another.

The room was sparse, like the rest of the house. He spent some time cautiously exploring his wife's belongings, feeling a twinge of sadness at the sight of her beauty paraphernalia in the bathroom and the books she'd been reading on the nightstand. Her clothes, however, were surprisingly impersonal. But then, that was her style. Classic.

Not like Colleen in her long peasant skirts and tight t-shirts, cowboy boots and short shorts. He smiled. Anything but classic, Colleen was an original.

Looking around the room, he realized he could do this now. He went down to the basement and brought up a few boxes. Some things were hard, like the jewelry he'd given her, and the scent of her shampoo almost brought him to tears, but he continued packing her things, the remains of their life together.

He studied the pictures on the dresser of the two of them together, laughing and leaning toward each other. They'd had good times, at first. When had they become so driven?

No sense assigning guilt. They'd been in it together then, but he was on a new and different path now.

One thing was clear—he couldn't live in this house.

When he had packed up the bedroom, he pulled out his phone and made a call.

* * *

The next morning, Alex pulled his BMW into a parking space beside his dad's Mercedes in the private parking lot at the lawyer's office. His grandfather had wisely chosen an impartial third party to handle his estate, a friendly rival of Porter, Porter & Porter.

He was a few minutes early and noting Daphne's car wasn't there, decided to wait for her to arrive. He didn't want to face his father alone. It wasn't cowardice—his decision was made and nothing his dad could say would change his mind—but a little moral support wouldn't go amiss.

Less than a day back in the city and the emptiness was already stifling the energy that had flickered to life during his weeks at the lake. But he was clear on his decision.

He'd have to find a place to live, his dad wouldn't let him stay on at the lake house once he knew he was pulling out of the firm. And he had to find work, hopefully something he felt passionate about, something that would get him out of bed every morning eager to greet the day.

And he wanted to give a relationship with Colleen a solid try. His eyes glazed over as he remembered their energetic lovemaking two nights before. No, he wasn't nearly finished with that woman. She breathed life into everything she touched, and she'd touched him, touched his heart to the core. He was going to go back and try his damnedest to make it work.

He didn't notice Daphne pull into the lot until she tapped on his window. When he got out of the car, his back was straight and his held head high. He was ready to defend his dream.

Inside, his dad was pacing the wood paneled hall. "Where have you been?"

"Hello to you too, Dad."

Alex's mother stood up from her seat on a chair along the wall and came to greet him. She seemed smaller than he remembered, her skin too big for her bones. Her normally fine eyes were puffy and red. He reached for her and she came into his arms. Gratefully, willingly. Did his father ever think to give her a reassuring hug? Her father had died, damn it, and Alex would have bet she hadn't been given any time to grieve. Not on their world tour.

"Hi Mom. I'm so sorry."

"I'm sorry I wasn't here with him in his last days. I'm just glad that you were."

His father made a show of looking at his watch. "Let's move this along. We have to get back to the office."

"I'm not going back to the office, Dad."

Like a Hitchcock film, time and space seemed to kaleidoscope as he waited for his father to answer.

"You can't spend all summer at the lake house."

"I am going back to the lake. For now, maybe forever, I don't know. What I do know is I'm not coming back to the office. I'm tendering my resignation, effective today."

His dad's eyes bulged and the veins in his cheeks engorged with blood, but his jaw stayed firm. "Nonsense. I know you had a couple of rough years, but it's time to snap out of it."

"I am coming out of it. And I've realized I don't want to be a lawyer. Never really did."

"It's not a matter of what you want, it's your heritage."

"I have another heritage Dad, up at the lake. That's where I want to be, not stuck in an office in the city for the rest of my life."

"What on earth are you going to do, dear?" his mother asked, sounding more intrigued than upset.

"I don't know, Mom. Maybe work on boats. Old boats."

His father sputtered. "There's no money in that."

Alex thought of how happy he'd been lying in Colleen's arms in the creaky old bed at the cabin. "I don't need a lot of money. I can live simply."

His father drew a deep breath. "Don't expect any help from me."

Alex looked him in the eye. "Believe me, Dad, I don't."

His father turned on his heel and walked into the office at the end of the hall.

Daphne punched her brother in the shoulder as she walked by. "You go, Tiger."

His mother was watching, a bemused smile on her face. Alex crooked his elbow and she put a delicate hand on his arm. "You know, dear, I never thought you were cut out to be a lawyer. You're smart enough," she hastened to add. "But you don't have that ruthless streak. Thank goodness."

Alex smiled down at her. "Let's go in and hear what Granddad has to say."

* * *

Alex staggered out of the lawyer's office an hour later, his mind reeling. He stood in the hall for a moment staring sightlessly at the floor, rubbing his hand across his forehead as he tried to process what he'd just heard.

His mother followed him out. She put a hand on his arm and when he looked up, he saw she was smiling.

"Come by for lunch before you head back, dear."

He kissed her soft cheek, smelling the powder and faint, flowery perfume she'd worn since he was a kid. "I will."

His dad stopped in the doorway and gave Alex a searing look. "Well, you got what you've always wanted. I hope you're happy."

Alex checked his feelings, and grinned. "I am. Really happy."

But then he frowned at a new thought. "If you've always known that's what I wanted, why did you press me to be a lawyer?"

Forced was more like it, but Alex had to take some responsibility for his decisions. After all, it was his life and he shouldn't have let other people, his dad and Liz, talk him into something he didn't want to do. He felt lucky to be getting a second chance.

"As an adult, you don't get to do whatever you want. Being a lawyer is a responsible position in society. That's what's important."

Suddenly Alex wondered what his father would have done if he hadn't been so worried about being responsible. He tried to think of something else, but no, his dad was a lawyer through and through.

"I know you meant well. It was right for you, just not for me."

Daphne gave her dad a little shove from behind. "Blocking the doorway."

His father moved down the hall to join his mother, and Daphne barreled into Alex's arms. "Wow! I wasn't expecting that!"

Alex hadn't been either. He'd thought his grandfather might leave him a chunk of cash and maybe, if he was lucky, one of the boats. But Granddad had left him the whole friggin' island and everything on it.

He'd said in the video he'd left with the lawyer that the summers Alex had spent on the island meant so much to him, and showed him that Alex was the one who loved the lake as much as he did. He was sure Alex would put the lake house to good use. And he added a cash bequest to help with the maintenance which, as he said in the video, "was a buggar."

Good old Granddad! He'd left Daphne his town house and their mother the balance of his considerable estate.

"Dad's pissed that Granddad left you the lake house. Although why, I don't know. He never liked going up there."

"I know. The timing is perfect. I thought I'd have to get another place to live, because Dad wouldn't let me stay on the island once he realized I wasn't coming back to the firm."

"What's her name?" Daphne asked, a sparkle in her eye.

Alex tried to look innocent.

"Oh come on. There has to be something more than

those owls you told me about."

Alex's shoulders relaxed for the first time since he got to the city. "You're right. Her name is Colleen." He frowned. "We fought just before I left though, so I don't know how she feels about me right now."

Daphne's forehead pinched in concern. "What did you fight about?"

Alex took a deep breath and shook his head. "I don't know. I think we both just suddenly pulled back. Things were moving pretty quickly. But that's because she's so amazing. So full of life. It's been years since I've been as happy as I am when I'm with her."

"That's wonderful. And what are you going to do up there? You can't really be planning to be a fishing guide."

"No, that was just to help Dusty for a few weeks, although I actually am enjoying it."

Daphne wrinkled her nose.

He laughed. "What's not to like? Out on the water, spending hours every day fishing, hanging around the marina on my days off—did I tell you she works at the marina?"

Daphne shook her head, a skeptical smile on her face.

Alex grew thoughtful. "There are opportunities up there. You just have to know where to look."

Chapter 15

On the day of the EPA inspection, Colleen arrived at the marina at her regular time to find Pete pacing on the dock.

"There's lots of time," she said. "He's not getting here until ten o'clock."

"I know. Too much time. I wonder if he'll make a decision on the spot, or what?"

"I don't know. I guess they've got to walk the land and see what's what."

But they both knew what was what. Pete had gone over the contract again and told her it was not a done deal, the provisions on the contract were on until tomorrow and stipulated "logging on the land."

The ache in her stomach grew worse by the hour, but she was part of this now, no pulling out. Pride and fear sat on opposing shoulders like angel and demon, each whispering in her ear. She vacillated between hoping the environmentalists would win and wishing she'd kept out of it completely.

To quiet both voices, she busied herself filling the pop machine on the dock.

The ache in her chest was harder to ignore. Alex, her partner in crime, had disappeared without a trace. Dusty had been by to get gas and when Colleen saw the familiar green and white Cutty pull up to the dock, her heart leapt into her throat. Then it sank like a stone when she recognized Dusty at the wheel. He'd told her Alex had gone to Seattle and he wasn't sure when he'd be back.

Colleen wondered if it was 'when he'd be back' or 'if'.

She'd been too pushy, a common problem for her, and had driven him away. What right had she to try to organize his life? She should have minded her own business and just enjoyed his company while it lasted. Hadn't he said he was planning to stay? If she'd kept her mouth shut it might all have worked out. Now she'd never know.

At eight o'clock, her mother's red SUV pulled into the parking lot. Colleen felt a spike of adrenalin as the Hiking Hannahs piled out. In cargo pants and a colorful headband, Stephanie looked every bit the activist she'd been for decades as she crossed the parking lot to Colleen.

"What do you think will happen?" Colleen asked.

"Well, if the EPA does what the Sierra Club committee is pushing for, they'll call a moratorium on logging on this side of the lake." Her eyes sparkled with excitement.

Colleen didn't feel nearly as happy. "Then the whole deal would be off."

"We can only hope."

After that, protestors arrived by the carload. The handful of people at the initial meeting had mushroomed into dozens, all ready to spend as long as it took until this thing was settled. Excitement crackled in the air. Word spread that a Seattle TV station was sending a remote.

The rain had washed the road dust off the big leaves of the maples and as the sun peeked through the clouds, the forest glistened. Many of the protestors had placards and a couple of guys slung a banner between two trees that read, "Save the Northern Spotted Owls." Mothers with small children in tow bragged to each other they'd go to jail if necessary. Fiona said she'd chain herself to a tree, and Colleen's eyes widened when she saw the heavy chain in her hand.

As the minutes ticked by, Colleen's stress level rose. She

really wished Alex was here. He'd understand how she felt.

Finally, the truck with the EPA logo on the door pulled in, the prospective buyers right behind in their big, black SUV. The protestors rallied in a straggly line along the edge of the forest.

It was fortunate Colleen wasn't one of the negotiators because she couldn't have spoken past the baseball sized lump in her throat. The EPA man, clipboard in hand, studied the protestors from the cab of the truck, then mouthed the words, *Oh, shit,* picked up his phone and made a call. When he was finished, he shrugged and got out of the truck.

Colleen's heart wasn't in the protest anymore and she watched the proceedings from the doorway of the store with Pete and Roseanne. She couldn't look them in the eye. "I'm so sorry guys."

Roseanne, bless her heart, put an arm around her shoulders and gave her a squeeze.

Pete said gruffly, "Wasn't anything else you could do."

The EPA man was obviously a, "just the facts, Ma'am," kind of guy and wasn't going to get dragged into an emotional community fracas. Matthew and Stephanie came forward with the head of the Sierra Club delegation and they conferred with the EPA inspector and the prospective buyers.

The main buyer kept his poker face in place while they spoke. The other man jingled his keys in his pocket and paced. In a bit of comic relief, he stepped in a mud puddle in his shiny brogues, then hopped around the parking lot shaking his leg, getting a disdainful look from his partner for his trouble. But even that wasn't very funny.

Gone was Colleen's earlier elation at the possibility of saving the land. Her eyes kept swinging to the dock, expecting Alex to roar up in *The Millie*. But that didn't happen.

The delegation led the inspector up the trail into the woods leaving the protesters waiting in the muddy parking lot. A soft misty drizzle began to fall and looked like it was here to stay.

The buyers got into their car to wait. Pete wandered out to talk to the locals, now milling around in the parking lot. "Roseanne's got coffee and cookies for you all inside. No sense standing around in the rain."

He returned to the store with the protesters in tow, everyone saying things like, "Sorry to have to do this Pete," and, "You know this isn't personal."

"What will be will be," was all he said.

A while later another van, this time with a satellite dish on top and a local TV station logo on the side, pulled into the parking lot. The decibel level of discussion surged. Fiona and her husband went out to talk to the reporters who followed them into the packed, steamy store to interview the protesters while they waited.

The rain started to fall in sheets.

It seemed like a lifetime before the hikers came back. The EPA guy stopped at the black SUV and spoke to the buyers who rolled down a window to confer. Then he got into his truck and both vehicles drove away.

"Here they come," someone called. The room fell silent.

The local delegation trudged through the muddy parking lot toward the store. Matthew was grinning, wiping away the water that dripped onto his face from the soggy brim of his hat, but he didn't say a word.

Stephanie stopped in the doorway and looked at the expectant crowd. She waited while the cameraman and reporter got into position, then she smiled, a broad grin.

"They are Spotted owlets, and Matthew Swallow has found another possible nest at the far end of the property." A cheer went up. People slapped each other on the back in celebration.

Pete and Roseanne kept a brave front as the protesters dispersed. No retirement nest egg for them now, just hard work to keep the business afloat until the next buyer came along.

But Colleen had seen the sad look they exchanged when Stephanie broke the news, and she vowed she would stay at the marina, without pay if need be, until they worked this thing out.

Chapter 16

Alex dipped the oars into the water, maintaining a steady rhythm as the old rowboat made its way along the shore. The rain had passed and the sky was mostly clear. He breathed deeply, letting the hint of ozone still in the air clear away the residual anxiety from his head and the city air from his lungs.

The family of ducks were cruising in the tall reeds. He had always been cautious around wildlife, but now a new sense of ownership shimmered in his chest. This was his place and he would take care of it.

The low sun illuminated the lonely figure sitting on the Murphy dock. Colleen stared at the water, looking dejected and alone.

His heart pounded and the blood rushing to his chest, leaving his extremities weak. What if she wasn't glad to see him? He'd left without telling her why. Their argument a week ago seemed pointless now, and so long ago.

He hadn't called. They'd never exchanged phone numbers. It hadn't seemed necessary in their days at the lake. Besides, he wanted to talk to her in person. But a week was a long time to be missing in action and he was worried she wouldn't talk to him at all. And what had happened about the sale of the marina? He just hoped he wasn't too late.

She looked up as he neared, but didn't move, didn't smile, just watched impassively as he drifted in. They stared at each other in silence, then she said, "I didn't know if you were coming back."

"I'm sorry. I should have let you know where I'd gone."

"Dustin told me. Anyway, you don't owe me any explanations, it's just..."

The boat bobbed on gentle swells beneath him and in the still air, the sound of voices drifted down from the house. It sounded like a party. "Just what?"

She thought for a moment. "I shouldn't have pushed you. It's your decision if you want to be a poet or a fishing guide or whatever. Things were fine the way they were."

He smiled, remembering their exuberant lovemaking the night before he left. "Just fine?"

It was hard to say, but he thought she was fighting a smile.

"More than fine," she allowed. But then she pushed out a sigh and her shoulders dropped. "Then, besides the fact that you *disappeared*—" she put the same accusatory spin on the word that Daphne had mastered, "—things kind of went to hell in a handcart."

It seemed like an opening, so he took a chance and threw her the line before he drifted away. She caught it with one hand and pulled him in.

He climbed out of the boat and quickly tied up, then sat on the edge of the dock beside her, hip to hip, shoulder to shoulder, careful not to press against her. "What happened?"

"You were at the meeting. It all played out just as they planned. The EPA guy came this morning. Everyone showed up at the marina—way more people than at the meeting. A television crew and everything. The buyers were there too. But it turned out they weren't going to be the buyers after all because Matthew had gone back on his own and found another breeding site at the far end of the property."

"That's amazing."

"It is amazing, and wonderful, but it means there's not a chance in hell they can get permission to log that land, which is also wonderful except that now Pete and Roseanne have lost the sale, and they were really counting on it. And where were you?"

He took her hand in both of his to slow her down, to apologize, but more than anything, because he wanted to touch her. "They were reading my grandfather's will. Once I got back to the city there were things I had to do. Deal with my job—"

"I thought you quit your job—"

"I have now. And my house—"

"You have a house?"

"—and way too much family stuff."

After a heartbeat she said, "So you're going back."

Where did that come from? "No. Of course not. I'm staying right here."

Her face brightened. "Really?"

He nodded and her hand relaxed in his. She leaned against him and rested her head on his shoulder. "I really needed you there today. It wasn't exciting at all. I felt so guilty, so responsible for ruining the deal. Now Pete and Roseanne will have to work forever, or until someone else wants to buy it. And how many people are going to want a rundown marina?"

Alex smiled. "There might be one or two."

She didn't seem to hear him, just sat up straight and said in a determined voice, "So I decided to stay on there until they find a new buyer. It's the least I can do."

They were silent for a moment, then she said, "You own a house in the city?"

He nodded. "I put it on the market. I never liked it

anyway."

He could see the wheels turning in her head.

"And what were you saying about your job? You never really told me what you do. Besides being a poet."

"I'm a lawyer." He braced himself, half-expecting to end up in the water. Not everyone liked lawyers.

She didn't push, but she pulled her hand out of his and fisted it on her hip. "What?"

He nodded. "Guilty as charged. My dad's firm. His dad's before him. My sister's one too."

She laughed. "Poor baby."

He shook his head sheepishly. "You have no idea. Granddad was my salvation, to be able to come here every summer, to fish and water-ski and learn to work on the boats. He was always a stickler about the boats."

Colleen nodded, her voice softened. "I know. He used to bring them to the marina."

He took a deep breath. "But apparently my visits meant a lot to Granddad, too. He left me the boats."

"Oh Alex!"

"And the lake house." Her eyes widened. "The whole island actually."

She threw her arms around his neck and he closed his eyes as relief washed over him. It was going to be all right.

She let go and sat back. "I'm so happy for you. Are you going to open a practice here?"

"Not on your life. I want to work on boats. Nice boats. Old boats."

She nodded. "Like *The Queen*."

"Exactly." He slid his arm around her waist, the last tension in his chest loosening when she leaned her head on his shoulder. He dropped his face to the top of her head and took a deep breath. She smelled like flowers and fresh mountain air.

"The island isn't really a convenient location for running a business though," he said into her hair. "It should really be somewhere people can drive to, in their cars, pulling their boats.

"I want to buy the marina."

Colleen spun around and put her hands on his shoulders. "Are you serious? Can you afford it?"

Enough of this sitting side by side. He pulled her onto his lap and wrapped his arms around her. "I think I can swing it. I never wanted to be a lawyer. It was my dad's dream. It's time I go after my own dream. And this is it. I've never been as happy as since I came here."

Then she gave him the welcome-home kiss he'd been hoping for.

When they came up for air, he asked, "Am I forgiven? You're not disappointed?"

"Disappointed! Are you kidding? I was afraid that if they couldn't find a buyer, I'd be working for Pete until I was forty."

He sat very still. "So, you don't really like working there?"

"I *love* working there, but it doesn't pay very well, and it's seasonal. I couldn't afford to stay forever."

"Too bad." He kissed her again. "Because I was hoping you'd stay on." He kissed her neck, just under the ear, and she murmured, *mm-mm-mm,* deep in her throat.

"I could probably manage a raise." He nibbled his way down to her collar bone. "And, you know, benefits."

She pulled away and gave him a playful slap on the side of the head. He laughed and ducked, but continued. "If you stayed on I'd write you a sonnet, especially if you wore those short shorts to work every day."

"I told you. I'm not that kind of girl." She jumped to her feet and pulled him up with her. "Come on. Let's tell Pete and Roseanne."

"They're here?"

"They're the guests of honor."

Alex threw back his head and laughed. "God, I love this place."

* * * * * * *

I hope you enjoyed meeting the people of Fortune Bay in **Lake of Dreams**. *Keep reading for the sneak peek at Jake and Sarah's story, eight years later, in*
Summer of Fortune.
Publishing date, June 17, 2016.

If you did enjoy this introductory novella, nothing would help me more in this new world of online marketing than a review, no matter how short, on the site where you purchased this book, or on Lake of Dreams goodreads page. A good review is worth its weight in gold.

Then, join me on my website for previews of the upcoming three Fortune Bay books.

Thank you for reading,

Judy Hudson

www.judithhudsonauthor.com

Summer of Fortune
Book One in the Fortune Bay Series
By Judith Hudson

Chapter 1

When life hands you lemons, you make lemonade.

My motto in life, thought Maddie Tedesco when her ex-husband's name popped up on the caller display. But really, how much lemonade did one woman have to drink?

When she answered the phone, his greeting was brief. "Maddie."

"Mark."

They didn't spend much time on pleasantries anymore. He was Jenny's father though so, when he asked to speak to their daughter, Maddie handed her the phone.

"Hi Dad...Everything's great...No, nothing planned ..." Jenny's voice rose to a shrill crescendo. "I'd love to... Sure, we'll talk." She put down the phone with a satisfied smack.

Listening from her post at the kitchen sink, Maddie's jaw clenched. How many times had Mark disappointed their daughter, making plans and then not showing up? If he did it again, she'd wring his neck.

Plastering the smile on her face that she'd perfected in the ten years she'd been divorced, she turned to her daughter.

"Mom. You'll never guess what. Dad asked me to spend the summer with him and Kate."

Maddie's cheeks stiffened as the smile melted like a chalk drawing in the rain. Jenny would graduate from high school next spring and, thorny as it may be, this could be her last summer at home. By asking Jenny first, Mark had undermined Maddie's veto again, swooped in like a fairy godfather and invited Jenny to Yuppiedom-by-the-sea.

Maddie leaned heavily on the counter. "Do you want to go?" Her voice sounded hoarse.

"Of course I do. Why would I spend the summer in this stifling attic when I can be in a mansion by the beach?"

Hardly a mansion, but Mark's beautiful Seattle Craftsman-style home *was* right across the street from the beach, and a far cry from Maddie's third floor walk-up.

"How about it, can I go?" Jenny asked.

"I don't know. I have to think…"

"Come on. This is my chance to move up in the world. I don't want to end up like you—living in an attic when I'm thirty-five. "

"Hey, it's cozy."

"And working at a job I hate."

"I don't hate my job," Maddie objected. But Jenny had pretty well nailed it. Being a receptionist at an art gallery—or an administrative assistant, as Maddie preferred to call it—wasn't her dream job, but it did pay the rent.

"You could have fooled me." Jenny put her hands on her hips in a perfect imitation of Maddie. "You always say I can achieve whatever I want if I just put my mind to it. 'Go after what you want,' you say. Well, I want this. A chance for something better."

Maddie stared at her daughter. Jenny stared boldly back, her long, straight, reddish-blonde bangs hanging in her eyes. Maddie's hand itched to reach out and brush them aside but she resisted. Instead, she turned away, picked up a scrub pad and began scouring the sink. "We'll see."

As she sensed Jenny watching her from the door, her shoulders stiffened and her hand slowed in the sink.

"It's clean enough Mom," Jenny said softly. Then, like a wraith, she vanished into her room.

Maddie put her hands on the counter, dropped her head and sunk her weight into her arms. It was unnerving when Jenny caught her cleaning. And really, was cleaning so bad? Jenny seemed to think so but Maddie could think of things that were much worse.

She had promised herself she'd be a good role model for her daughter, the best mother ever. Fun yet patient, adventurous yet wise. Her daughter's best friend. And it had worked, at first. But sometime during the last few years, their relationship had gone from BFFs to combatants. Mark could offer Jenny a life Maddie couldn't hope to achieve. What if Jenny didn't want to come back after the summer?

She glanced at the clock, six thirty, time for a family-fix.

In the living room she turned on the TV and the *Family Ties* opening scenes appeared on the screen. As always, the reassuring music was an anchor for her turbulent emotions. Turning up the volume, she went back to the kitchen to start dinner.

These were the families she'd grown up with: The Seavers, the Cosbys and her favorite, the Keatons. Elyse Keaton had been her dream mother, had taught her more about being a mother than her own mom ever had. Despite being an architect, Elyse always had time for the family.

Maddie longed to be part of a family like that and had tried to give Jenny the best home she could. But obviously her best wasn't good enough or Jenny wouldn't be so eager to go and live with her dad.

Elyse's voice echoed in her head. "*Of course Jenny wants to connect with her father. Don't you remember what that was like?*"

She remembered all right. The longing, the wondering, the ache in her chest. At least Jenny knew who her father was.

Maddie let out a sigh that left her hollow. The weight of inevitability settled on her shoulders. Of course Jenny should go to her dad's. It was the right thing to do.

Go after what you want. She *had* said that—and meant it. Maybe in this case, being a good mother meant letting her daughter go.

Wiping her hands on a dish towel, Maddie called Jenny back into the kitchen. Maddie's heart twinged when she recognized the suspicious look on her daughter's face that pretty well epitomized their past year together.

She tried to smile but her cheeks felt like hard plastic. "I've made a decision. You can go to your dad's for the summer."

Jenny let out a whoop and threw her arms around her mother. The irony wasn't lost on Maddie that this was the first spontaneous hug in so long, and all because she was letting her go.

Jenny rushed to her room to call her friends. Maddie took a deep breath and turned back to her magazine recipe. She'd splayed the chicken on a roasting pan— apparently it baked faster this way—and now crumbled the dried rosemary and thyme between her fingers, sprinkling the herbs over the bird. She added salt and pepper and, as the final notes of the Family Ties theme song died, slid the chicken into the oven.

Then she turned off the TV, grabbed a rag and started to scrub.

So bite me, she thought. *It helps me think.*

Jenny was right about her job. What happened to her dream of being a photographer? When she and Mark had first married, she was just starting out. A creative fire had burned in her belly. Some interesting freelance assignments came her way that hinted at a promising career, but once she was married and a mother, Mark wanted her at home. She'd resisted at first, but somehow the jobs petered out until, without even a puff, they completely disappeared.

After the divorce, she'd been happy to get the job at the gallery, but ten years in, it felt like—settling.

The only bright spot that she could see in this whole situation was that now she could spend the summer working on her photography. Maddie's boss Eileen had never supported her work as an artist, but there was another gallery owner, Tori at the Edge, who had expressed interest in her black and white darkroom art.

Maddie threw down the duster and pulled her portfolio out from behind the couch. If she was going to make lemonade, she might as well get started. She'd show Tori her photographs tomorrow.

* * *

The following evening, dusk had fallen and her boss Eileen was long gone when Maddie finally closed the heavy glass gallery door and turned the key in the lock. The neon signs of gallery row reflected in the wet pavement as she fought the stream of people hurrying home from work and headed to Pioneer Square. A historic district popular with tourists, it was a mecca for new galleries like the Edge.

Good name, the Edge. Tori had a knack for marketing. Maddie had never been able to get out there and flog her work. After ten years of putting her dreams on hold, it had only gotten harder as her faith in herself slowly ebbed away.

Time to make a change.

As the downtown hustle fell away and she entered the relative quiet of the streets around the Square, her boots sounded a determined rhythm on the pavement. The rain had eased to a heavy mist that fogged the streetlights and frizzed her hair. The trees showed a faint haze of green and she could smell spring in the air.

In a week the city would be in full bloom. Other years, she would have had her camera out and been snapping atmospheric nighttime shots as she walked. Lately though, the city had lost its magic, and tonight her mind was focused on her meeting with Tori.

Rounding a corner, Maddie's heart lurched at the outline of a hunched figure on a dark storefront step. Tucked in out of the rain, a woman sat with an upturned hat on the ground in front of her.

Time slowed and the ground felt like quick sand beneath Maddie's feet. *Please, no.*

The woman turned to face her. It wasn't her mother. The hand squeezing Maddie's heart loosened its grip and she blew out a sharp breath. Taking a bill from her purse, she dropped it into the hat. "Get yourself something hot to eat," she said gently, even though she knew the chance of that was virtually nil.

As she walked away, her shoulders twitched as she tried to shake off the adrenalin buzz. Now that her mother lived in the city, in the back of her mind Maddie knew that Cindy could pop out anytime, anywhere, and turn

Maddie's world upside down.

Suddenly she was standing under Tori's hand-carved gallery sign. Time to get back on track.

She prided herself on being fearless, most of the time. But this one-two punch of her two worst fears, meeting her mother by surprise and showing her photographs to a gallery, had turned her knees to mush. She forced the thoughts of her mother out of her mind—*that wasn't her, just a sad old woman*—and pulled her thoughts back to the job ahead.

Showing her photographs always felt like she was stripped naked and flattened on the gallery wall. She closed her eyes and breathed deeply. *In, one, two. Out, one, two...*

She'd read about this breathing technique in a magazine. It was designed to ease panic attacks and, she discovered while reading the article, apparently she had them.

By the time she reached ten, her heart rate had slowed. Pulling a tube of crimson lipstick out of her shoulder bag, she applied it with a sure hand. The ritual always gave her courage, allowing her to channel the kick-ass, take-no-prisoners femme fatales from the black and white movies she loved.

She rolled her shoulders. *Showtime*. Tugging open the wooden door, she climbed the steep gallery stairs, the envelope with her prints clutched in one clammy hand.

The smell of fresh paint rolled down to greet her and she stopped at the top of the stairs to admire the dark red paint, the color of borsht, that Tori had applied to the walls in preparation for the next show. "Wow."

A muffled voice called out through an open door at the back of the room. "Somebody there?"

Shaking the raindrops off her jacket, Maddie crossed the gallery and peeked into the office. Tori's ample rear end, sheathed in leopard-skin pants, stood in bold relief as she bent over a stack of paintings.

Maddie smiled. "Busy?"

Tori stood up and shook her head, her short pixie-cut hair sticking out in all directions, as usual. "Tuesday night is Art Walk and we're going to be swamped. Not that I'm complaining." Her gaze dropped to the envelope in Maddie's hands and her face lit up. "For me?"

Nerves hit the panic button in Maddie's brain and her fingers instinctively tightened on the envelope. Tori tugged it out of her hands with a wicked grin and spread the gritty eight-by-ten black and whites of the city and its people out on the table.

"These are fantastic. Great contrast. Your darkroom work adds so much drama; I just want to rub my finger over those velvety blacks. People are eager for black and whites again. They're tired of photoshopped specials."

Maddie's shoulders relaxed. It was going to be fine.

Then Tori asked, "Weren't these in your show last year?"

Maddie's chin came up, her eyes widened. "You saw the show?" That venue had been more of a gift shop, not a real gallery at all.

"I read the article in *The Caller* and stopped by."

Maddie nodded, her mind racing. "It brought in a lot of people. I only have a few pieces left. I was hoping you could put them up sometime."

Tori shook her head. "I don't know kiddo." She tapped the prints on the table in front of her. "These are great, but they're old work. I was hoping you'd bring me something new."

Gritting her teeth, Maddie attempted to smile. That was a problem. She didn't have any new work. Shortly after last winter's show, somehow, somewhere, she'd lost her muse. The urban shots on which she'd built her reputation—such as it was—didn't inspire her any more. The spark had died leaving her a gutted candle, a hollow puddle of wax. She had hoped getting a few pictures into a gallery would give her the push she needed to start moving in a fresh direction. Tori was right though. She couldn't put up old work.

Maddie gathered the prints into a pile. "I understand."

Tori fisted her hands on her sturdy hips. "I don't think you do. You need to get your ass out from behind that counter at Eileen's and get behind the camera where you belong. These are great, but it's time you had your own show. Right here. My October artist just cancelled. Can I pencil you in?"

Maddie's eyes widened. Her own show. *Her* work up on the walls. The chance of a lifetime. The star falls and breaks her leg and Maddie Tedesco steps in.

But October was only six months away. Could she possibly get a new body of work together by then while still working full time? Eileen would hit the ceiling...

But what about her resolution to be a better role model for Jenny? Wasn't the best way to go after what she wanted, too?

Although Tori was several inches shorter than Maddie, she managed to put her arm around Maddie's shoulders. "You know, sometimes to get the good things in life you have to take a leap of faith. Like I did last year when I opened this gallery."

Maddie heard Elyse Keaton's voice whisper in her ear. *Time to make lemonade, dear.*

Okay. She grabbed the last lemon and squeezed.

"I'll take the show."

"Good, I'll pencil you in."

"No. You can write it in pen. I'm not sure if I'm jumping or if I've been pushed, but I'm definitely taking the show."

* * *

Elbows on the kitchen table, Maddie rested her head in her hands, the bass rhythm from the floor below beating a backbeat to her thoughts.

What was she thinking, accepting Tori's offer? How could she take the show?

How could she not?

Even after she and Mark had split up, she had continued taking pictures. Preferring the compositional challenge of black and white, she had set up her darkroom in the bathroom, taking Jenny inside when she was too young to be left in the apartment alone.

But Jenny was almost grown now, taken care of for the summer, and this show—*a solo show*—had dropped in her lap. How could she pass it up? Especially with the long, lonely, rest-of-her-life looming ahead of her. This was her chance to get back in the game.

If she was being perfectly honest, she knew why she'd stayed working for Eileen for so long. It was safe. Secure. Didn't demand she put herself on the line. Now, though, she was afraid she had traded that safety for her daughter's respect, and lost her own creative spark along the way.

That was something Mark had never understood, that to her photography was like breathing. It was how she experienced the world and without it, she only felt half alive. She might as well just breathe into the top half of her lungs, never feeling the satisfaction of filling them completely. Without her photography as an outlet, numbness had slowly crept into her extremities.

Outside her tiny kitchen window, the setting sun gilded the snowy mountain tops that peeked up from behind the downtown. She'd never been to the Olympic Peninsula before. Had never had the time or money for any kind of holiday. She needed something to jumpstart her creative juices though. And leaving the city and heading into the mountains? That would be different. That would be new. Surely then she would find her muse.

Take the summer off to work on the show? That was crazy. Wasn't it? Could she afford it? Maybe just barely.

This would be something truly worthwhile to spend her nest egg on. An investment in herself, in her future. A fresh start.

If she was going to make the most of this chance, she couldn't hold back. She had to be all in.

Chapter 2

Three weeks later to the day, Maddie dropped Jenny at Mark's house to finish the school year. Eileen had hit the gallery's vaulted ceiling when Maddie told her she wanted to take the summer off to work on the show, but once Maddie found an art student to fill in for the season, things had tumbled into place. As if the universe was giving her a big thumbs-up. She just crossed her fingers that her job would be waiting for her when she got back.

As she pulled away from Mark's house, father and daughter stood on the stone front steps, waving goodbye, Mark's arm draped casually over Jenny's shoulder. Maddie watched them recede in the rear view mirror and—*oh, great*—Mark's new wife Kate joined them on the steps. The stone front steps of the beautiful heritage house they had lovingly restored. The perfect family in the perfect house. Maddie shook her head and dragged her eyes back to the road. How could she ever compete with that?

Two hours later, Maddie stood on the deck of the giant car ferry as it plowed across Puget Sound. Her Nikon digital to her eye, she zoomed in on the forested slopes of the Olympic Peninsula as sunlight caught the rugged, snowy peaks. She snapped a shot.

The salt air whipped around her, clearing away all doubt. *This is why I came. This is what I am looking for.* Her new muse was a forest nymph. She just knew it.

But she needed a cheap place to rent for four months, because she planned to be back in the city by Labor Day to work at the gallery and welcome Jenny home. Assuming her daughter wanted to come home after, as Jenny had put it, her "summer in paradise."

That was what worried Maddie most, that Jenny would decide to live with her father. She had to win back her daughter's respect and that meant making good on the show.

It had been years since she'd been on her own. It felt exhilarating—and weird like she had lost her anchor with no timeline to follow and no one to look after. Adrift and disoriented, she needed a home base and she needed it soon. With high hopes and a few apartment leads in her pocket, she drove her aging station wagon, fondly known as The Beast, off the ferry in Bremerton.

Two days later, still looking but starting worry, Maddie pulled into the lot of a fast food diner. None of the places she'd looked at were at all possible. All lacked any hint of inspiration and, in some cases, even basic hygiene. This was no closer to her forest nymph than Seattle.

Tapping an agitated rhythm on the Arborite tabletop, she studied the map. Roads circled the Olympic Peninsula close to the shore with a few smaller roads heading up the river valleys into the mountains.

Further inland was probably less expensive, an important consideration since in the end, unable to bear the thought of other people using their dishes and sleeping in their beds, she hadn't sub-let the Seattle apartment. Online from home, she hadn't seen any inland rentals but maybe she could find a cottage somewhere. Nothing fancy, just a place to sleep, a small kitchen, and a bathroom where she could set up her darkroom.

She could see it in her mind's eye—nestled in the forest, dripping with atmosphere.

A young waitress stopped at her table, pad in hand.

"Road trip?"

"Sort of. If you could go anywhere on the peninsula for a holiday, where would you go?"

The girl chewed the end of her pencil, then stabbed a finger at a lake in the center of the map. "Fortune Bay on Majestic Lake. It's beautiful, right in the mountains. My uncle has a hunting camp there and I go up sometimes in the summer. I love it. He's right on the lake."

Maddie ordered a burger and studied the map. Fortune Bay was a dot on the map at the end of the road running up one side the lake. Isolated, probably rustic and picturesque as all get out. As good a place to start as any.

She ate quickly, then climbed back into the Beast and headed west.

An hour later, she crested a ridge and pulled into a rest stop at the top of the pass. Majestic Lake hugged the curves of the valley below, surrounded by forested mountains, some still tipped in snow, that rolled out to the horizon. Pulse racing, she pulled out her camera, first taking wide-angle shots, then zooming in on the shore.

Goosebumps prickled on her arms. Something down there pulled her like a magnet.

Back in the car, she flew down the mountain and through the town of Majestic, following the signs toward Fortune Bay. Fifteen minutes later, all spent driving through a dark forest worthy of the Brothers Grimm, the lake winked at her again through the trees and, soon after that, a sign welcomed her to Fortune Bay.

Maddie drove slowly though the town; a handful of streets lined with faded, crayon-colored houses and, at the end, a general store. The road continued along the lake from there, in and out of forest and field until, a mile out of town, the trees opened up and a fallow field, bordered by tall evergreens, ran down to the lake.

A cabin peeked through the trees, the crumbling chimney stretching toward the sun as if preening for her attention. Maddie's foot hit the brake and the Beast shuddered to a halt. She inched ahead to the spot where a lane disappeared into the trees, and pulled over to the side of the road. From here, the building was hidden in the forest but a hand-painted sign nailed to the trunk of a massive fir tree announced that the cabin was for rent. Someone had written a phone number across the bottom of the sign but, having been disappointed before, she decided it couldn't hurt to take a peek before she called.

She jumped out of the car, ducked under the rope strung across the drive and headed down the lane. A gusty breeze swirled branches overhead and the air had the faintly medicinal tang of lake water and cedar.

At the end of the drive the cabin was waiting, with weathered white siding, an overgrown flowerbed and a porch facing the lake thirty feet away. The wind blew white caps out on the bay and rocked the limbs of the towering evergreens protecting the cabin. Maddie framed a shot of the porch in the viewfinder and clicked.

It was perfect. Charming and oozing with inspiration. She pressed her lips together in excitement. She had found her muse, but could she afford it?

Up on the porch, a sun-bleached couch stood under a picture window and, cupping her hands to the glass, she peered inside. The room was dark. Dead flies lined the sill. Definitely deserted and possibly right in her price range.

Then something moved at the back of the room. Something big.

Maddie stifled a scream and leaped back off the couch, landing on her butt on the wooden porch floor.

The inner door flew open and a man stood in the doorway.

"Looking for something?"

* * * * *

*If you would like to keep reading, you can order **Summer of Fortune** from all online retailers in eBook or trade paperback form.*

For news of upcoming releases and giveaways of The Fortune Bay books, join my Readers Group on my website at ***www.judithhudsonauthor.com***.

Thank you for your support,
Judy Hudson

The Fortune Bay Series

Lake of Dreams
Get this prequel novella free when you sign up for
my mailing list at *_bit.ly/freeFB-e-book*
*Colleen's back on Majestic Lake for the summer, living in the
cabin, helping out at the marina and looking for romance with Mr.
Right. A fun introduction to the series.*

Summer of Fortune
Book One
*Maddie wasn't looking for romance. Could a summer of freedom
change her life forever?*

The Good Neighbor
Book Two
*Sean hates to see Frankie and her father estranged. He'd give
anything to know where his own daughter is.*

Home for Christmas
Book Three
*Blue's carried a torch for Louise his whole life, but this time he's
not sure he can wait around to pick up the pieces.*

Family Matters
A Sequel Novella
*Things are at a low ebb for Frankie and Sean. Be sure to read The
Good Neighbor and Home for Christmas first!*

Starting Over
Book Four
*After a horrific motorcycle accident, Marshall's life seems to be
over—until Lily knocks on his door.*

Copyright

Made in the USA
Monee, IL
01 November 2024

69093736R00074